CAL SMYTH

WRONG WAY AROUND

iPonymous Edition 2 Published 2013

First Published in 2011
By iPonymous publishing Limited
iPonymous Swansea United Kingdom SA6 6BP

Design: www.GMID.co.uk

A CIP record for this book
Is available from the British Library

ISBN 978-1908773265

www.iponymous.com

As a teacher in Serbia, Japan, Mexico, Italy and the UK, Cal has met wanted criminals and exiled intelligence agents. He has dealt with various visa scams and been given 24 hours to leave a country about to be bombed.

Married twice, he lives with his son.

PROLOGUE

Colin ignored the food on the breakfast tray as he snatched at the postcard that came with it. The postcard picture depicted a topless beauty reclining on a white sand beach, turquoise sea lapping onto the shore. Phuket was in italics at the top, looking like it was pronounced "Fuck it", which seemed appropriate. Colin flipped the card over.

There was no message, just Colin's name and prison address. It wasn't her handwriting, but he knew it was from Linda. This could prove that she was still alive and that he hadn't killed her. He had to speak to his lawyer.

In his excitement, he accidentally clattered over the plastic tray. It brought him to his senses, dashing his sudden dream of freedom. Before he even called the guard, he knew it would be no use - she was too clever to leave fingerprints. Staring at the postcard, Colin pictured Linda far away on some Thai beach while he rotted in his cell. As his euphoria died, he wondered how it had come to this:

You're supposed to do the crime first, then go on the run – we did it the other way around. Maybe that's where we went wrong…

CHAPTER 1

They met in a bar in Shinjuku, Colin there with a group from Hello Tokyo, the magazine he'd just done a fashion shoot for, pretending to be happy. Truth was, he'd had his fill of Japan - it just wasn't his cup of green tea.

The bar was called London Calling, as retro as you could get. A screen silently showed clips from Blow Up, Peeping Tom and Performance – red double-deckers and black cabs sliding into view. A jukebox played The Clash, The Kinks and Saint Etienne - names of famous streets and bridges drifting into hearing.

The Japanese men loved the place because of the western hostesses that worked there. Especially once they'd had a few Kirin beers and their true lewdness came out.

The group's hostess sashayed over to them in a body accentuating silk green dress, tray of snacks in one hand. Striking a pose, she swished her blonde hair off her face, which of course sent the Japanese men wild. Shinji, one of the magazine editors, leered:

'You are very b–e–a–utiful.'

The others all laughed at his deliberate English pronunciation. The blonde hostess smiled a fake smile as she placed bowls of shiny nut-shaped puffed rice on the low table, to go with the half-drunk beers. At first glance she looked like just another girl in the wannabe Monroe mould.

Colin looked at her face more closely, for photographic purposes he told himself. It was the flexibility of her face that was fascinating. She had a mouth that could laugh easily but also curl in hate.

He should have known then he was in trouble.

The hostess finished serving, turned and saw Colin looking at her. Not needing to put on a fake smile for the western customer, she met his look, both of them holding it before she turned and went on her way.

Shinji saw the exchange of looks, turned to Colin:

'You like her too huh? Leave some girls for us! You have already one waiting.'

Shinji gestured to the porcelain-faced model sitting impassively next to Colin, who he'd been shooting all day in Yoyogi Park, under the cherry blossom. Shinji turned back to the rest of his gang:

'You know why he gets so many girls?'

The others shook their heads in unison, letting Shinji answer his own question:

'Because he is Englishman and he has very big penis!'

The group burst out laughing, drinks spluttering from their mouths. The more beer they drank, the more roles reversed, thought Colin, the Japanese men getting louder as the English man sat back, observing.

Colin finished his beer, stood up and said:

'Guys, I'm off.'

'Oh no, only joke, stay for more beer.'

'I'll send the hostess over on my way out.' Shinji

gestured to the model:

'But look, you leave her very sad.'

Without looking, Colin left the table. At the bar, the blonde hostess was filling up her tray with more beer to be served to another table. Colin paused by her:

'Pretty busy eh?'

'Uh huh.'

'Your fan club over there is ready for their next round.'

'You're not?'

'What, part of the fan club or ready for another beer?'

She carried on putting glasses of beer onto the tray as she answered:

'Either.'

'I'm going now, but I'll come back later. What time do you finish?'

'Why,' her Mancunian accent came out in full as she sarcastically said:

'You want to walk me home?'

Colin let that hang there for a few seconds, enjoying their banter:

'No, but I'll buy you a drink.'

The hostess started to walk off with the tray, then briefly paused, smiling over her shoulder:

'Midnight.'

Colin was waiting for her when she came out of the bar, leant against the wall and twisting an old train ticket in his fingers. He had steady hands, but if they weren't holding a camera, he didn't know what to do with them.

Over her dress, she had a lightweight wrap-around jacket with a wide belt. Colin was in his usual jeans, T-shirt and hoody zip-up. He might have been a fashion photographer, but he didn't care about his own fashion. Years taking photos of other people's appearance had that effect so much of it was a facade.

As the hostess walked on by, she could only half prevent a smile:

'So you're serious?'

'About what?'

'Walking me home?'

'I'm a serious guy.'

'You don't look it.'

'That's what my mum told me. Said son, you'll never have a serious relationship because you're never serious.'

Colin moved off the wall, walking alongside her:

'Anyway, I didn't say I'd walk you home, I said I'd buy you a drink.'

'But if I miss the last train, I'll have to wait until morning.'

'We'll get one on the way.'

Colin spotted a can dispensing machine up ahead, jogged up to it and gestured with his hand:

'What will it be madam? Green Tea? Asahi Beer?'

'A true romantic, beer.'

Colin put money in the slot, took out two cans of cold Asa- hi, gave one to the hostess. They held up their cans to each other, said "campi", the Japanese for "cheers", and knocked back a hit. The hostess lowered her can:

'I'm Linda by the way.'

'Colin, nice to meet you.' Linda laughed:

'That's my surname, Linda Collins.'

'Or Colin's Linda.' She laughed again:

'What about you, what's your surname?'

'Crosswell.'

'Like the teacakes?'

That's what everyone said. Colin tried not to roll his eyes. Crosswell, the famous English bloody teacakes. Usually he said "yea, same name but no relation". But he shrugged, told Linda the truth:

'Yea, it was my Grandfather's company. It was supposed to be passed down but my dad spent all the inheritance. What was it George Best said – he spent nearly all his money on drink and women. The rest was wasted. That's how my dad saw it too.'

Colin paused. Was he going to tell this girl he'd only just met his whole life story? Next he'd be recalling the day his grandfather was taken to hospital with a heart attack. Thirteen years old, he'd been holed up in his room, headphones on so he didn't have to listen to his dad have sex with the local barmaid while his mum was day shopping in London, spending money they didn't have.

They didn't know he was in the house as he'd secretly skipped school and sneaked back in. From his window

Colin saw the barmaid leave, but he stayed motionless in his room until the phone rang, making him jump. He let it ring, but his dad didn't answer it. When the phone started up again, Colin cautiously went into the hallway. He peered into his parents' bedroom and saw his dad passed out so he picked up the phone.

Colin nodded silently to the voice from the hospital, the person unsure if Colin had understood the situation. But he was just trying to work out what to do. If he woke his dad up it would be obvious he wasn't in school. But if he didn't, they might not see his grandfather before he died. He called a taxi and shook his dad awake. Half-plastered, his dad didn't question why Colin was there or helping him stagger out to the taxi.

Time they got to the hospital his grandfather was dead, so Colin's decision had been in vain. But it didn't matter as neither of his parents ever asked what he'd been doing at home.

Colin shrugged off the memory and said:

'The company was sold off years ago. They kept the name but it's nothing to do with the family anymore. So if its money you're thinking of marrying me for, forget it.'

'Must be something else I'm after then, because you've made me miss my train.'

Linda's mouth turned into a wide smile. Colin wanted to kiss that mouth.

A second later he did.

Colin and Linda didn't finish their cans of beer. Nor did they make it to her place. It was late and all public transport had stopped, only extortionately priced taxis remaining, so they went down to the Love Hotels - a bizarre arrangement of architecture, fake gothic structures at odds with the surrounding modern business district.

Most of the places were already full, but one still had vacancies. In the reception area there were screens displaying video stills of all the rooms. For the romantics, there was a Roman style room with 4-poster bed and paintings of voluptuous women, naked and reclining. You wanted something more funky, there was a seventies disco room, complete with ceiling mirrors and glitter ball. Or if you preferred it more hardcore, there was an S&M style room, the bed caged by red metal bars.

The only room still lit up and available was the traditional Japanese room, so that's what they had. Any room would have done. They hardly got each others clothes off, straight down onto the low bed, Linda unzipping his jeans, Colin pulling her knickers down - neither noticing the "tatami" straw matt flooring or mirror that went along all four walls at just above bed height.

Second time, Linda rolled Colin to the side and straddled him. Taking her time now, she pulled her dress over her head, revealing small but pert breasts, with bright pink nipples. As she started to ride him, Colin grinned and cupped them with pleasure:

'Cup cakes I could eat.'

Linda though stopped riding, taking offence:

'Are you saying they're small?'

Before Colin could reply, Linda grabbed a pillow and pressed it down over his face. He slapped the mattress in submission and she relented. Colin got his breath back:

'I'm saying I could eat them with tea - a Crosswell speciality.'

Linda's half-turned mouth reverted to a smile as she forgave him, her tongue darting inside his mouth as she started moving her hips again.

The third time, both sitting, they saw their reflections in the mirror and couldn't stop looking, stars in their own show. They looked good together, matched each other.

He didn't pretend to be the world's most handsome, but he had gleaming blue eyes and a chiselled jaw. Losing his hair a bit on top, but at six foot one, most people didn't see that, especially in Japan.

She did pretend to be one of the world's prettiest and with her green eyes and high cheeks she pretty much pulled it off. Her pubic hair was dark, showing that she was a fake blonde, but not many would see that. He hoped so anyway, presuming Linda didn't go with just any guy and that her passion was mutual. She'd made a lot of noise and left scratch marks on his back. He was pretty sure it was genuine.

Ten in the morning, the hotel reception phoned the

room, telling Colin and Linda it was time for them to leave. Shiny eyed from too much sex and too little sleep, they went to a café for breakfast. Colin looked at the menu:

'Problem with Tokyo is you can't get a decent cup of tea. I mean tea should be brown, dark brown, not green.' Linda joined in:

'And if you ask for toast, they'll probably put bean paste on it and roll it up.'

They laughingly agreed that Tokyo was great for noodle bars but not so hot for cafes.

Over "American coffees" and "French croissants", the nearest they could get to what they wanted, Colin asked:

'Where are you from originally?'

She looked at him quizzically. Wasn't all night sex enough for this guy? What else did he want to know, her favorite colour? She decided to amuse him:

'I grew up in Man-ches-ter,' laying on the accent, 'left when I was eighteen.'

'I grew up with that whole Manchester scene, used to love the Stone Roses, Happy Mondays, showing my age.'

'Twenty eight, twenty nine?'

'Twenty nine.'

'Me too.'

'And look, after the same number of years, we've ended up in the same place in life. How did you end up here?'

'I came out as an English teacher just to get the visa, and then I left immediately to get a job as a hostess.

Loads of money for simply smiling and letting Japanese men ogle you. And hey, seeing as I get that on the train everyday anyway, I might as well get paid for it.'

'Makes sense to me.'

'What about you, what are you doing here?'

'I don't know really. I started out on the cruise ships as a photographer, got trained on the job. For a while it was great, travelled all over the world, had a great time, had a really good mate called Vinnie - he sorted my visa out for here…'

Colin looked at Linda. She'd told him without hesitation about how she'd got a job on false pretences, so he guessed it was okay to explain:

'…you probably know, you've got to have a degree to get a work permit for Japan and I never finished university, so Vinnie printed me out a fake degree. But the reason I'm here, I got bored of being on the boat, so when we docked in Tokyo, I stopped here, got a job as a fashion photographer.'

'Bet you get lots of girls after you.'

Colin smiled in fake modesty. Linda continued:

'When I first arrived, I saw all these ugly male English teachers, all with beautiful Japanese girlfriends.' Colin frowned, taken aback:

'You saying I'm ugly?'

'You're an exception.'

'Everyone always wants what they haven't got. The Japanese girl wants the Western man, and vice versa.

Don't see too many Japanese men and Western women together though.'

'It's a strictly look but don't touch policy, thank God.'

'Don't know if it's true, but they do have this whole inferiority complex, that Western men, you know…are bigger.'

'I wouldn't know…so do you have a girlfriend?'

'Yea, and yes she's a model I photographed, but she doesn't have a mouth like yours.'

'I'll take that as a compliment.'

'What about you?'

'Uh huh, he's a pilot. I call him when I'm in the mood and he flies on in.'

Colin looked down, went silent. Linda pouted at him:

'Hey, don't be sad. He's okay, but he hasn't got a mouth like yours.'

Colin looked up at her, tried to be cool:

'I'll ditch mine, if you ditch yours.'

'It's a deal.'

With wide smiles, they shook on it.

They saw each other every day, before and after work, the rest of the day just an interlude between sex. Alternating between each other's flats, they would wake up to make love. He would go to his job, wait for her to finish hers, then they would rush back home for more.

On the escalators to the platform in Tokyo central, Colin always stood one step below Linda so that they

11

were the same height to kiss.

In the last train out of central Tokyo, Colin's height and Linda's blondeness stuck out, drawing unblinking stares from Japanese business men over the top of their manga porn. Or a gaggle of teenage girls in long white socks, high-step shoes and shirt skirts would giggle and whisper "gaijin, gaijin," the Japanese for "foreigner".

Oblivious, Colin would tell Linda how he'd been thinking of her all day. Linda would raise her eyebrows – yea, she knew what he'd been thinking about. He'd start to protest it wasn't just that and she'd cut him off with a kiss, her hand surreptitiously rubbing against his groin.

Both their flats were on the outskirts of Tokyo, towards Funabashi. Colin's place was old style Japanese with tatami floor, sliding paper doors and a square bath. For the first month, every morning when he'd risen from the thin futon, he'd cracked his head on the low doorframe. And when he had a bath, he had to sit with his knees at head level. Apart from his camera equipment he kept the flat minimalist, or miserablist as Linda called it. Tokyo was a haven for techno gadgets and Colin had often frequented Akihabra, or Electric City as it was known.

Linda's place was in a modern block, still with tatami flooring, but containing a shower and mod cons. The walls were adorned with photos of Linda striking poses on various beaches. On the floor were beach flip-flops from Ibiza where she'd worked as a tour operator, over the chair was a sarong from Bali where she'd recently been on holiday.

In her flat one morning, as Linda came out of the shower, Colin held up a blonde wig:

'What's this?'

'It was an eighties night, I went as Madonna. When I was little I used to listen to her all the time, especially "Material Girl". Linda put on the wig, started gyrating in her bra and knickers as she sung:

'I am a material girl, living in a material world.'

She took a stance, made a pout. With his hands, Colin made as if to take her photo.

'Must have played that song every day for about a year. Used to drive my dad mad – he was this big time socialist, probably still is, don't talk to him much. He couldn't believe it. He wanted a socialist world and his little girl just wanted to have fun and make money... which is pretty much what I've been doing ever since.'

Linda took off the wig, and said:

'What about you, bet you'd look good in it.'

Colin let Linda put the wig on him, Linda ordering:

'Don't move.'

Naked apart from the blonde wig, Colin stood still while Linda held up the Samsung Smartphone he'd bought for her in Akihabra, Linda clicking a photo. Linda smiled:

'If you ever become famous one day, I'll sell it to the papers...you know who you look like? Jack Lemmon at the end of Some Like it Hot. I love that film.'

Colin wasn't sure what he thought about looking like Jack Lemmon in drag, but he was also trying to think who Linda looked like with the wig on. It wasn't Madonna, but some American actress, he just couldn't think of her name.

That night, they couldn't wait until they got into Linda's flat, doing it fast up against the railing outside, hands all over each other. Suddenly, Linda started slapping Colin on the shoulder. Colin turned to see a teenage boy watching them, his hands down his pants, masturbating furiously with a lewd grin.

Linda and Colin quickly disentangled themselves. But before Colin could turn on the boy, he ran away. Linda was already in the flat, furiously stepping out of her skirt, turning on the portable air con. Even at night it was too hot to wear anything inside. Colin came in, shutting the door behind him:

'That was embarrassing.'

'God, I can't stand this place any more. We're surrounded by perverts. Everywhere I go, looked at for being a gaijin and a blonde.'

Colin was surprised by her anger, but shrugged:

'Then why don't we go somewhere else?' Linda smiled:

'You know where I've always wanted to go? Cancun. You know, in Mexico. Have you seen True Romance? It's my favourite film. At the end, that's the beach where they run away to.'

'Okay, why not.'

Linda kissed him:

'And you know what else, if we go to Mexico from here, the plane more or less goes past Las Vegas. What do you think, should we stop over, try our luck in the casinos?'

Colin hesitated, taking a breather from her sudden enthusiasm. She smiled a little, letting him take his time. Was he ready to run with her? Did he have the balls? Colin's flickering doubt was that it was all her ideas rather than his. He batted it away. Wasn't that just male pride? He smiled back:

'Sure, let's do it.'

He should have seen what was coming next.

CHAPTER 2

They got married in a love chapel, the in-house photographer as witness. It was another of Linda's impromptu ideas, put to Colin on the plane's descent into Vegas at night – the vast neon-dotted bowl within the surrounding desert below. She'd turned wide-eyed from the window, slid a hand onto his thigh and looked him in the eyes. How could he turn her down?

The chapel was fifties Americana, Colin opening the gate in the white picket fence for Linda and providing his arm to walk through the wooden awning doorway. For a second, Colin was taken back to all the old noir films he'd watched late at night on BBC2 as a teenager.

Linda had wanted Elvis - the seventies one, in white jump suit - to be there too, but he was fully booked. It seemed that particular Elvis was real popular. There were other Elvis's available at short notice but they were pretty second rate so Linda gave up on the idea.

Colin didn't comment but was glad it was just them. Not just because fifties style chapel and seventies era Elvis were at odds, but secretly afraid the marriage was becoming more about Linda's image of it than their desire to be together forever.

In Vegas, if you looked good, people treated you good. And in their hired outfits – Linda in white dress, Colin in stream-line suit they did look good. The initial on the spur idea had turned into a day's hard shopping, Linda deciding they might as well do it properly.

After scouring several shops, Linda had fallen in love with the perfect dress – a mix of traditional veil and modern body hugging design. Colin had to admit, she looked incredibly sexy in it. Already tired from traipsing after Linda, Colin wanted to get his clothes shopping over as soon as possible so let her dress him up. Placing his white shirt collar outside the black suit jacket, Linda took a step back and took an admiring glance at the tightness around his groin.

As they strolled down the Boulevard, they were stars for the day, everyone shouting "congratulations", several people stopping them to ask if they could take their photo. After posing a couple of times, Linda said they needed their own photos.

With Colin's Nikon back in the hotel, Linda took out her Samsung Smartphone and got someone to take photos of them in front of a replica Trevi Fountain, below a small version of the Eiffel Tower by the side of a fake Venetian canal. Who needed to go to Rome or Paris or Venice, when you could just take a picture as if you'd been there?

After a celebratory ice cream, given to them free, they went into one of the casinos. As they approached a slot machine, a fat woman bowled over, handing over a dollar coin:

'Here, a lucky dollar for the newlyweds, it'll bring you luck.'

Linda thanked the woman, put the coin in the slot, pulled the handle. Three apples lined up and a payout of several silver dollars came clattering out. Colin and Linda exchanged looks. He said:

'What do you think, this is just the start.'

Linda nodded:

'This time next year, we could be millionaires huh?'

That night, in a room at the top of The Venetian, with the blinds open, Colin and Linda stood looking out at the neon- lit strip below. Linda turned to Colin with a seductive smile:

'Think we should consummate our marriage?'

'It'd crossed my mind.'

Linda pressed him to sit in an armless chair:

'Not yet.'

She sat in the chair opposite and slowly started stripping off her wedding gear, Colin getting hot inside his suit as he watched. Down to her wonderbra and g-string, Linda pouted at Colin:

'Come on, don't be shy.'

Colin followed suit, taking his off. Linda unfastened her bra, eased her knickers off. Glancing between the Vegas view and Colin, she started touching herself, her legs squirming and breath getting faster. Caught up in her excitement, Colin stroked himself.

Naked and too aroused to wait any more, they rose to meet each other standing. Their hands tentative as almost every touch sent them both into orgasms. What they didn't realise was that really was the climax.

From then on, it could only go downhill.

Their Cancun honeymoon started off in the ocean-front Hilton, overlooking an expanse of white sand and green sea. With her blonde hair and green eyes, Linda matched the beach as she lay down on the recliner to get tanned. Colin gestured at the water:

'You not coming in?'

Linda pulled a face:

'You joking? I'm here to get nice and brown, not do something strenuous like swim.'

Linda closed her eyes, basking in the sun while Colin made his way down to the sea on his own. Almost wilting in the heat before he even got there, Colin plunged into the first wave.

It had been a couple of days and Colin was starting to get restless. All Linda wanted to do was lie on the beach to get brown. As beautiful as the sea was, he was bored of swimming on his own.

It wasn't even that great for swimming, the already huge waves enlarged by all the speedboats and water skiing that went on. There were coral tours and deep-sea diving on offer too, but Linda wasn't interested. Maybe she had a point. For a place to relax in the sun, there were an awful lot of activities touted.

Bobbing in the water with an eye out to make sure he didn't get decapitated, Colin took in the line of modern hotels. Cancun was a resort for the just about, or maybe even pretend, wealthy. If you were really rich, you had your own super yachts anchored in St Tropez. But if you'd saved up for the year, you could tell your friends how you'd gone deep-sea diving in the Caribbean.

Colin had a feeling Cancun itself had two sides to it. Along the wide, palm-lined road from airport to hotel he'd seen Mexican workers unload a palm tree from the back of a battered old truck – the line of trees as recent as the tarmac. And investment obviously hadn't reached out to the airstrip yet, the plane landing between dense overgrowth on what seemed like an earth runway.

For some reason, these thoughts troubled Colin. Coming back out of the water, dry by the time he reached Linda, he stood over her:

'Hey, we better start looking for work, if this is where we're going to do it.'

'Oh come on, aren't we on honeymoon?'

'Yea, but don't want to get caught out do we.'

'I suppose not. Give me another day.'

Leaving Linda on the recliner, Colin went into the Hilton to find out if they needed a photographer. The head of staff looked at Colin sceptically:

'No, sorry, we already have our own.'

Colin guessed he could hire himself out to tourists, but he wasn't used to going freelance. On the cruise ships and with Hello Tokyo, it was all in-house with equipment provided. Sure, he had bought his own stuff, but he'd sold most of it before they left Tokyo. All he had with him was his Nikon semi-pro. He could hardly walk up to tourists with that in hand and ask them if they wanted their picture taken.

A day later, they downgraded accommodation, moving from the Hilton, further towards town. Although called Oceana, the hotel they moved to was further from the sea, twenty rooms in a square around a pool. A step down from the golf ranges and ocean front of the Hilton, it catered for younger, less rich clientele. Sitting by the pool, Linda asked:

'So how much have we got left?'

'Not much.'

Linda didn't understand:

'We left Tokyo with loads.'

'Yea, but we spent it on the stop over in Vegas, the wedding, the hotel, the dress and suit…'

Linda pouted:

'Aren't you happy we got married?'

'Of course I am. I'm just saying Vegas cost us. If we'd walked from the tables when I'd said, we'd be sitting pretty…'

Linda frowned at him then relaxed yawning, removing her bikini top, determined to get an all over tan.

'Well until you set yourself up, I'll get a bar job.'

She stretched, arching her back, pointing her nipples at him. He liked that, though was unsure about her doing it in such close surroundings. Glancing over his shoulder, he caught a couple of guys quickly looking away.

In the evening, Linda asked the hotel manager if he knew of any jobs going and got a similar response to the one Colin had received in the Hilton:

'Can I give you some advice? In Cancun, foreigners come to stay in the hotels as holidaymakers, not work in them. There is cheap Mexican labour for that.'

A few days later, Colin and Linda moved into Hostel Cancun in the town centre. The pockmarked roads and run-down streets were even further from the ocean front and golf ranges. With a view of a decrepit-looking cinema that was only open at weekends, showing movies they'd already seen in Tokyo, the small room had no air con, but if you opened the window it just let in hot air, not to mention the smell from the overflowing metal bins below.

Waving a handmade fan at her face, Linda sat despondently on the bed, sulkily watching the Mexican version of Who Wants To Be A Millionaire? She couldn't understand the high-pitched Spanish, but got the gist.

It didn't matter which country or even continent you were in, everywhere had the same TV programmes, just in a different language. X Factor Mexico had been on the night before. That was good to watch. There'd been a guy in a sombrero that'd juggled balls then taken out a gun and shot them while they were in the air. Linda hadn't been back in Britain for a few years, but she bet you didn't see that on BBC1.

Standing at the window, Colin turned his gaze from Linda watching TV. At least she'd turned over from the soap-opera set in the Mexican equivalent of some middle-class home, where the overacting vied with the hysterical voices. The dialogue was incomprehensible but the plot seemed to evolve around the maid with huge tits having an affair with the man of the house. Strangely, it was when the maid's cleavage got a close-up that Linda switched channels.

The cleaners had just been and unblocked the toilet, but the room still smelt of unflushed shit. In the Hilton, Colin hadn't had to think about where to put the toilet paper as the hotel was properly modernised.

But as they'd downgraded, he kept forgetting you had to put it in the bin otherwise the toilet systems couldn't cope when you flushed. In both the Oceana and Hostel Cancun he'd blocked the toilets and had to apologetically tell reception.

Lost in reflection, Colin was thinking how their downward journey mirrored his childhood. As his dad had lost more and more money, they had constantly downsized.

He'd been born into a place called Fawley Manor, in the Oxfordshire countryside. His grandparents lived in the manor house itself, Colin's parents given the huge converted barn as a wedding present. Colin had vague memories of being happy there, his grandfather taking him for rides through the grounds on a golf cart, telling him one day it would all be his. But his dad soon sold up, causing a huge ruction as it let non-family into the manor.

They'd moved to a town house in Wantage, just outside Oxford. It was there he'd taken the hospital call. His grandfather's death should have provided the family with a bounce back up, but a combination of his dad already having spent his side of the inheritance and still with gambling debts conversely meant they actually had less now that his grandfather wasn't there to bail his dad out.

Colin vividly remembered the slide down Cowley Road, which led into Oxford. Moving house every few years, they'd started off in a semi-detached on the outskirts, gone inwards a few hundred numbers to a three-bed terraced, and then down to a two-bed almost at the end of the road in the city itself.

As soon as Colin had left home, his parents had downsized again – into a one-bed ex-council flat, though he'd never gone back to Oxford to see it. It was amazing that his parents were still together. He could understand why his mum tolerated his dad's drinking and womanising at the start as she was always off shopping or on holiday. Maybe it was out of habit, the two of them living off each other's torment. Who knew?

At least he occasionally phoned. Colin's brother never talked to their parents. After finishing his accountancy degree at the University of Winchester, he'd got a job in some bank in Singapore. Where he'd been banking and getting wanked off by rent boys ever since.

He phoned Colin up once a year on what he thought was his birthday, usually getting it a day early or late. The offer of a present was always the same, his brother would pay for Colin to fly out and stay for a few days. Promising to provide a full on service with the best girls in Singapore. Or boys, if that's what Colin preferred, his brother not even knowing his sexual preference.

They'd never been close. Four years older, his brother had gone to boarding school, just coming back for the occasional holiday. Their parents would have sent Colin too, but hadn't been able to afford it by then. It was the same with university fees, Colin's brother having his way paid. Not that it bothered Colin. Once he was eighteen, he just wanted away and seeing the advert for work on the cruise ships, he'd jumped on board.

Colin could have docked into Singapore, but hadn't even called his brother. He wanted to make his own way in the world and didn't want his brother's paid for services as way of making up for their non-relationship.

Turning from the window, Colin hesitated. He waited until there was an ad break:

'Maybe we didn't think it through properly.'

Linda squinted at him from the bed, her mouth a little slack:

'What do you mean?'

'Well neither of us speaks Spanish for a start, we hadn't set up any work before we came, and it's almost the end of the summer season.'

'So got any bright ideas?'

Colin grinned:

'I think we need to cut our losses. We've got just enough money to get a flight out. If we stay any longer, we're going to use that money up.'

She didn't laugh or even smile, but she knew it was true; her mouth was down-turned in a sullen expression:

'A flight where exactly?'

'London?'

Linda didn't answer. Colin didn't want to see her mouth curled the wrong way, he wanted the smile back. He tried to remain upbeat:

'We're both bound to get jobs in London. We'll sort it out and go from there.'

Linda's mouth was firmly closed, the ends of her lips pointing down. She got up and started sorting out the clothes in her suitcase. Not sure what it meant, Colin pressed for confirmation:

'Well, what do you think?'

'I'm packing aren't I?'

Colin strode over to her, taking her by the arm, his eyes searching for hers:

'Long as we got each other, we'll be alright.'

She'd heard it, but he couldn't see Linda's face, and he wasn't sure he wanted to.

CHAPTER 3

It was supposed to be when a person was tired of London, they were tired of life, thought Colin, but if you spent all your time either on the tube getting to work or working all hours to pay extortionate rent, it sure got tiring. Especially after all day taking photos for Tesco magazine – shot after shot of un-glamorous family wear on average looking models.

Linda was working as a receptionist in an office off Leicester Square, selling air con systems to other offices. It was right in the centre, but that didn't make it exciting. Even if she had the time and money to go out after work, she didn't have the inclination. After Tokyo and Vegas, the neon of Piccadilly was slightly pathetic.

They both worked long hours in dull jobs to pay the rent for a flat in untrendy Tooting, near the end of the Northern Line. Stepping out of the underground, Colin's heart sank as his fellow tube-going Tooting-dwellers poured out past him, everyone plugged into their earphones to escape the surroundings. It wasn't as poor as inner Cancun, but somehow more depressing. Weren't the dull terraced houses and grey skies what Colin and Linda had both escaped from years before?

They had less sex and more arguments. It wasn't the movie they'd paid to be in. On the occasions when they met up after work, Colin always felt that it was him who enforced their escalator ritual, Linda too tired to make sure she was a step above him for a kiss.

In Tokyo, they'd been locked on their own love island, oblivious to what went on around them. In London, they were isolated on an island of despair, not caring to talk to anyone else. They'd sent cards from Mexico, telling their parents they'd got married, but they hadn't got in contact on arriving back in England. Colin had even sent a card to his old mate Vinnie, who he knew was set up back in London, but he just never got around to calling him.

After a long day's shoot, trying to get kids to be still but natural for a family-wear shot, then the long journey home, first the Central Line from the studio in West London, then down to the bottom of the Northern Line, Colin trudged through the big sycamore leaves that had fallen all over the pavement on Totterdown Street and reached the mid-terraced house with three buzzers. At one time it would have been a house for just one family, but these days it was divided into three one-bedroom flats. In Tokyo, the flats were tiny, but at least they were purpose built. Colin walked up the thin carpeted stairs to the third floor flat.

Inside, Linda, her mouth drooped in a vacant expression, was watching Big Brother on an old TV left behind by the previous tenants. Colin sat down on the sofa next to her, looked at the TV, the live event of nothing happening to unextraordinary people, and couldn't resist making a comment:

'This is it eh, what our life has come to, just work then sit in front of the TV?'

'Oh thank you very much. What do you want, me to jump on your dick as soon as you walk in the door?'

'What do you think?'

'I try not to think. If I think too much I might jump off a bridge, after I'd pushed you.'

'So it's my fault?'

'Here we go, poor Colin.'

She mimed an imaginary violin, whining the accompanying sound before abruptly stopping:

'Look, can I just watch TV in peace?'

'What do you get from watching this anyhow?'

'I find it an interesting sociological study of how people act when they know there are cameras but they don't know where...Jesus, I don't fucking know, I just like it, alright.'

Linda rolled her eyes, ignoring Colin to concentrate on the TV screen. Colin shrugged:

'Sociological study? More like sociopath. If that guy wasn't prancing about on TV he'd be fucking dogs in Tooting Park. You want a cup of tea?'

Linda held up her empty cup and smiled as a way of making up. Colin took the cup and went out to the kitchen to make two teas. Rock and roll, he thought, rock and fucking roll.

The next night, Linda came home in tears. Colin had

finished work early and she was unusually late. She had her head down, so he didn't see she'd been crying as he said:

'Hey, kettle just boiled, you want tea?'

Linda didn't reply, brushing straight past him on her way to the bedroom. Colin followed her. Linda was sitting on the edge of the bed, head in hands. She shook her head as she explained:

'In Japan I got looked at all the time with my clothes on and got well paid for it. Here, in civilised fucking London, I get told to take my clothes off or lose my job. Un-fucking believable.'

Colin didn't understand:

'What are you talking about?'

Linda looked up, tear stains leaving black mascara lines down to her red lipstick.

'What am I talking about? That fucking wanker boss of mine is what I'm talking about. Made me stay late by giving me extra paperwork just as I was about to leave. When I finished it, I went into his office to leave him the papers and he fucking propositioned me, said that I could get higher pay, all I had to do was take my clothes off for him.'

'What did you do?'

'What do you mean, what did I do? I laughed, thought he was joking, refused of course. Then he said I had a week's notice.'

She shook her head:

'I didn't handle it right, let it go too far.'

Colin put his hand out to wipe Linda's tears away, but she pushed his hand away. He realised they were tears of rage not sadness as she said:

'I don't want pity, I want revenge on that wanker. I should have killed him.'

Colin nodded, thinking he understood, turned to go. Linda called after him:

'Where are you going?'

'I'm going to kill the bastard.'

And he really was going. To honour Linda? Maybe, but more in a rage at how their life had reached this point.

'You'd really kill him for me?'

'What do you think, I'm going to just let this go? If I don't do it, someone else will.'

'Come on, you want to go down for murder? There's got to be another way. We need to scare him shitless so he won't do it again.'

'But how do you know when you've scared him enough?'

That was one question, thought Linda, but there was another:

'And what's in it for us?'

'Eh?'

Linda rubbed her fingers together:

'Money, baby.'

The next day, Linda stayed late at work. When all of the

collections had been made, she stood outside the door of her boss's office, the nameplate stating 'Harold Robinson, Manager'. Linda was wearing her receptionist uniform of grey skirt and white shirt, but had chosen a deliberately short skirt and had the top buttons of her shirt undone, giving more than enough glimpse of thighs and breasts.

Linda coyly entered the office, leaning against the doorway seemingly awkward, but displaying a lot of her bronzed body. Harold was about to leave, just tidying up his papers. He was your typical picture of a small office boss – middle aged, overweight, balding. His podgy body at odds with his smaller limbs, his face blotchy from lunchtime wine. He darted his little piggy eyes at her, lust and disdain vying for each other.

Linda though was in seductive mode, contrite from the previous night:

'I just wanted to say I thought about yesterday, and I think I was wrong to walk out like I did.'

A big fat smile spread across Harold's face. He stopped putting his papers in order.

Linda pouted as she continued:

'I mean it's not too much trouble to take a few clothes off.' A bead of sweat dropped down Harold's face as he licked his lips, hoping his panting wasn't audible:

'I'm glad you came around to seeing things my way.'

'But just tell me again, what will I get if I take them all off?' Leering, Harold was happy to re-explain:

'If you take off all your clothes, you'll get a nice big pay rise.' And with that, Harold leant back in his chair, ready to watch – one hand on the armrest, the other adjusting his crotch. Suddenly Linda turned away in disgust, her mouth ready to spit, on her way out of the door. Harold couldn't believe it, shouting at her back:

'Do you want your job or not?'

'No I don't.'

'Stupid bitch.'

Colin watched the whole scene on Linda's Samsung smartphone they'd inserted into her shirt pocket. The top of the phone sticking out so that the tiny camera lens recorded the whole scene on film.

Smartphones had been all the rage in Japan and Colin had chosen the latest Galaxy S11 for Linda. She'd loved it but the only functions she'd used were text and camera so the outlay had seemed a bit of a waste to Colin. In London, she'd starting being like everyone else – downloading her favourite tunes so she could escape into her own musical world on the tube. Far as Colin could see, most people used their phones for playing games on.

In Tokyo, Colin had been up on his camera equipment and techno gadgets. Since being back in London, he'd lost his appetite for it all. He used the camera supplied by Tesco and had bought his mobile phone from them too.

Once they'd concocted their plan, Colin regained his techno enthusiasm. He bought a cheap laptop, also from

Tesco. My life, sponsored by bloody Tesco, he thought. But hopefully not for much longer. Using windows movie maker, Colin edited the video - deleting the part where Linda did the seducing, retaining Harold's terms of condition and insult. It was the most basic form of moviemaking, but it was so easy. Colin making a copy on the phone and laptop.

It was hard to watch another man being seduced by his wife, but he knew it was an act – an act of revenge, an act she was good at. And at least she was off screen.

The next morning, Linda stayed at home, while Colin went into Leicester Square. Next to Harold Robinson Air Con Supplies was Hot Girls Peep Show. A bored looking woman with tits hanging half out and wearing a bedraggled hair extension was standing in the peep show doorway. Colin stopped by her, asking:

'You don't know anything about old Harold Robinson next door do you?'

'Might do.'

'Make it worth your while.'

'Thought that's what I was supposed to do.'

Colin took out his wallet, held out a twenty pound note as he asked:

'He ever come in here?'

'Harold? All the time, he's a dirty old perv. Think that's why he has his office there. Seen how many receptionists he goes through, new one every month.'

Colin handed the woman the note. She took it, made as if to put it down her cleavage, but stopped and winked:

'Better not put it down there, might get lost. When you come back down, give you a free show if you like.'

Thanks for the offer, thought Colin, but he'd seen enough. The door to Harold's place opened to a set of stairs, the office on the first floor. The reception area was empty of receptionist, but full of boxes, 'Robinson Air Con' written on them.

The manager's office door was half open, so Colin walked in. Harold looked up from his desk:

'Sorry we're short of a receptionist at the moment, what can I do for you?'

Without being asked, Colin sat down opposite Harold, giving him a funny look. Harold shifted in his seat uneasily:

'Is this about the delivery to the unit in Hounslow?'

Colin had to smile:

'No, it's not about that.'

'Because the shipments coming at the end of the month.'

This guy was priceless thought Colin, telling him stuff he didn't even need to know.

'No, all I want to do is ask you a question. The receptionist you mentioned is my wife. Yesterday she refused to strip for you and now she no longer has a job. What would you call that?'

Harold's eyes darted between door and phone as he

started to sweat. Was this for real? Colin was easing into the role now:

'I'd call that sex-u-al har-ass-ment.'

Harold snorted:

'A fine kind of wife to have. She came on to me first.'

'That's not what she told me, or what she'll be telling the courts.'

Harold laughed:

'It will be her word against mine.'

Colin took the Samsung smartphone out of his pocket and held it up. Harold still acted unconcerned:

'Good bluff.'

'See for yourself.'

Colin held out the mobile, saying:

'Just press "play". And don't bother trying to delete it, we've already got plenty of copies.'

Harold was silent, no longer so sure of himself. Reluctantly he took the phone, pressed "play". The video came on, starting with Harold leant back in his seat, saying:

'If you take off all your clothes, you'll get a nice big pay rise.'

Harold started to react angrily:

'But that's not everything…'

'Save the violins.'

Harold's fat arrogance quickly faded, realising he'd been done. Colin drove the point home further:

'I've heard you've been through quite a few

receptionists. Maybe we could call them all up on the stand, see if they've got anything to say.'

Harold sat silently fuming. Colin pointed to the photo on the desk:

'That's a nice family photo. Is that your wife and daughter? Be nice to have everything out in the open in a nice big court case, being sued for sexual harassment…'

Unable to contain himself any more, Harold burst out: 'What do you want?'

'Her year's salary. Transferred into our account. I have the details with me. You can do it over the Internet while I'm here.'

'How do I know you won't use the video later?'

Colin took out a piece of paper, held it out, saying:

'We give you this signed contract, stating that she agrees as your former employee that she has no complaints about your employment and will never make a legal complaint against you.'

'Give me your bank details.'

'I'll dictate them to you. Turn the screen so that I can see you're really doing it.'

Harold turned the computer screen so that Colin could watch as Harold transferred money from his business account to Colin and Linda's joint account.

Transaction completed, Colin stood up to leave, gestured to the mobile on the desk:

'You can keep the phone, we'll buy a new one.'

Leaving Harold slumped at his desk, Colin turned and

walked out of the office.

As soon as Colin walked in the door of the flat, Linda jumped on him, pulling down his trousers and pulling up her skirt. They did it on the kitchen table, just like Jack Nicholson and Jessica Lange in the remake of The Postman Always Rings Twice, thought Colin.

The excitement was back.

CHAPTER 4

In the morning Colin went to the underground station to get the free Metro and the local shop to buy the Evening Standard. He'd quit his job with Tesco Magazine. He had a new job. A job called blackmail.

With music by The Stone Roses pumping out of the newly bought stereo system and coffees from Starbucks on the table, Colin and Linda took a newspaper each and looked through the jobs ads, circling any possibilities. It had to be a small company in central London requiring a receptionist.

After a few phone calls, an interview was lined up for one of the jobs, a small language school off Oxford Street. Linda dressed up in interview clothes fit for receptionist work. Still the office temp uniform of black pencil skirt and white shirt, but bought in French Connection rather than Top Girl, one step up. It no longer seemed to her like wearing a boring old uniform. It was costume as part of the act; Linda crossing her legs as she sat across from Colin, giving more than a flash of inner thigh as she finished off the role-play:

'So, when do I start?'

'Yea, that ought to do it. Hope you're going to put some knickers on though. Bit too much Basic Instinct.'

Linda winked:

'Don't worry, that was just for you.'

With it's grand sounding name Oxford Language School appeared to be in the hubbub of central London, but the only people it fooled were unwitting foreign students who passed by or desperate teaching staff. On the corner with Tottenham Court Road, the sign was on Oxford Street, but the entrance was around the side. Up worn-out carpeted stairs, the school contained several run-down classrooms, and desk chairs in urgent need of repair.

Linda took it all in as she entered the reception area. A sweet looking Japanese woman pulled a face of almost disgust when Linda said she was there for the interview.

Looking Linda up and down, the Japanese woman went to fetch Stephen Lewis, the owner and manager of the school.

Linda watched Stephen enter, trying to be casual as he looked at a file, a paunchy guy in his fifties with a full head of receding hair. He had attempted to hide the belly by wearing a loose shirt from Paul Smith and combed his hair back to make it look swish, when presumably he was covering up baldness. Just go for a jog and shave your head, thought Linda. Leering over his file at the passing Japanese female students, he obviously thought he was still hip with the kids. Inwardly shaking her head in disgust, Linda kept a smile plastered on her face as Stephen dropped the file on the reception desk and turned her way, inviting Linda into his office.

With the door shut behind them and both sat down,

Stephen leant back in his chair, giving Linda a thoughtful look:

'I have to tell you, I usually hire foreign receptionists, they know what they're dealing with.'

'Is that right? Well I've travelled quite a bit, as I'm sure you've seen from my CV.'

Stephen picked up her CV, giving it a cursory glance, his eyes scanning Linda more than the paper in his hand. Linda crossed her legs:

'I can see a lot of your students are from Japan. You'll see I lived there for a few years, teaching English as a matter of fact.'

'And now you want to work as a receptionist?'

'Lack of funds and a daddy who won't give me any.'

Linda's mouth went into seductive curl, green eyes looking straight into Stephen's. He said:

'I need someone as soon as possible, at the moment it's just being covered.'

'I'm very flexible; I can start when you want me to.'

'Well then, how about we start tomorrow?'

'I'll be here first thing.'

Linda rose up from the chair, skirt and shirt displaying just a hint of thigh and breast. She leant over to shake his hand, turned and left the office. Trying to remember to roll his tongue back into his mouth, Stephen watched her all the way out.

Back at the flat, Colin was eagerly waiting as Linda

breezed in with a fleeting kiss. Colin frowned:

'Hey, you okay?'

Flinging off her clothes as she made for the shower, Linda spoke over her shoulder:

'Sure, all ready to roll. Guy's a right lech.'

'Sounds perfect.'

While Linda showered, Colin watched, listening to her give the low down:

'Absolutely perfect. Should see him drooling over all the Japanese girls.'

'Sure he's going to go for a blonde like you?'

Linda gave him a look with half-closed eyes, putting it on:

'Do I need to answer that?'

'When do you start?'

'Tomorrow. No experience needed, which is not surprising considering what he's paying – monthly in arrears with no contract, one dodgy guy…Now can I have some privacy?'

Linda pulled the shower curtain shut. Looking through the curtain at the outline of her body as water poured off it, Colin opened his mouth, wondering if he should articulate his fears about what they were getting into, but changed his mind to think a little more on it.

Colin left the flat, to get the tube, Northern Line up to Tottenham Court Road. First he scouted the electric goods shops. It wasn't quite like Electric City in Tokyo, but he found what he wanted easily enough, the latest iPhone 4, complete with iMovie so that films could be edited on the phone itself. And an apple laptop to hook up to, ready to go pro with the blackmail movies.

Colin went to the pub opposite the Oxford Language School, paying over the odds for a bottle of imported beer. He got used to the iPhone, keeping an eye on anyone coming out of the school. After the evening class finished at six, first out came a flurry of foreign students, then a couple of English-looking young men, headed straight for the pub.

As the two men got their drinks, Colin listened into their conversation, one man saying to the other:

'That's another one gone.'

'Hey I'm probably the longest serving teacher in the place and I've only been there two months!'

'What a wanker, he didn't even pay her for the final week.'

'As soon as I can get a better job, I'm going, not even going to tell him, not as if he's going to pay me once he knows I'm going.'

'Seen anything?'

The second man got out a newspaper:

'Yea, have a look here. There's a couple of jobs going in St Giles, they're a really reputable school.'

'In Holborn, aren't they?'

'Yea, and they pay decently and you get a contract.'

Colin had heard all he needed to. And just coming out of the school, locking up, was Stephen Lewis himself.

Colin left his beer and followed as Stephen went down into Tottenham Court Road tube station. They went on the old Northern Line, but north instead of Colin's usual south, getting off at Highgate. Colin should have guessed Stephen would live somewhere like that.

Stephen turned into a three storey semi-detached house on Fitzgerald Avenue. Colin walked on past, catching sight of the children's swing in the garden. Perfect, not only was he a sleaze who tried not pay his staff, he had money and a family.

Linda started the job. Colin did further research. A week later and they had all the necessary details. Over pizza, Colin asked:

'You managed to check his accounts?'

'He's got a business one as well as his personal one. I don't know how much exactly is in either, but I've heard him do transactions over the phone, simply transferring fair amounts.'

'Okay, well I've got his family details. Wife and four year old son. She's already caught him in the act once before, with a Japanese receptionist. Told him if she ever caught him again, she's getting divorced and taking half the money.'

Linda squinted at him, smiling a little:

'How the hell did you find that out?'

'Talked to the au pair.'

'Oh, you talked to the au pair?'

'Those au pairs are something else. One beer and they're all yours, tell you anything you want to know, and lots you don't.'

'Where's she from?'

'Slovakia, the pearl of Eastern Europe. According to her. Misses her Babba and her clogs. Her Babba made the clogs and she used to go out dancing every Saturday.'

'How old is she?'

'Twenty one.'

'Pretty?'

'Yea, very.'

'What, you attracted to her?'

Linda stared at Colin, a mean look in her eyes. Colin backed away:

'Hey what is this, Spanish inquisition?'

'No, the Slovakian inquisition.'

'It's Stephen we're spying on, not me remember.'

Linda let go of the stare:

'So when do we do it?'

'Tomorrow, might as well get it over with.'

Colin got the idea Linda was making it out to be a bigger ordeal than she really thought it was.

'How much should we demand this time?'

'Let's stick to manageable figures. Same as before, a year's salary, easy figure for him to cover in the books and not make him cry too much.'

'Easy figure for you maybe. I'm the one in the eye of the storm. Don't you think we should squeeze a bit harder? You don't make an omelette without breaking eggs.'

'I've tasted your omelette, that's why we eat out. We don't want to spook him too much or he might flip. It's got to be something realistic, easily got and transferable. If we ask for too much, he'll panic.'

The next night, Linda stayed after all the teachers and students had left. She looked at herself in her compact. Not a blonde hair out of place. Green eyes like the sea. Lips to kiss. She blew one to herself.

She checked the iPhone was attached to the inside of her shirt pocket, pressed the record button, Colin having shown her how to do it as if she couldn't work it out herself. Did he think she was dumb?

Stephen was still at his computer when Linda entered his office. He looked up surprised, pleasantly so:

'Linda, thought you would have gone home by now.'

'I wanted to talk to you alone. I'm going to tell you something I've never told anyone before.'

Stephen slowly moved his hand away from the keyboard.

'Really?'

Stephen Lewis believed he was pretty cool. Okay he was hitting fifty five but he still had his hair and knew how to download apps onto his iPhone, just like the one in Linda's pocket. Though what he was more focused on was the glimpse of her pert breasts in the shirt opening.

If he played this right, he was pretty certain big daddy was about to get some. Linda looking him in the eye:

'I can't keep it from you any longer. I love big men, and you're a big man. You know what turns me on?'

'Jimmy Choo shoes? Am I right? What size are you? I tell you, if you're good to daddy, he'll hook you straight up.'

God, that was good he thought. Linda standing there, her hand on her hip:

'A girl is always going to get herself into some scrapes for her Jimmy's, but what I really like is being mauled by a big bear. Are you a big bear Stephen? Can you see yourself doing some mauling or am I in the wrong office?'

Stephen tried to think of some new quip, but his brain had seized, his mouth dry. He gestured dramatically and managed to say:

'Has everyone gone?'

'Uh huh.'

'What do you want me to do?'

Linda seemed to think it over as she lifted her skirt to reveal lacy knickers:

'I want you to walk towards me like a bear, saying "I'm going to rip off your knickers you dirty slut."'

Stephen couldn't wait any longer. Standing up from behind his desk, he beat his hands on his chest, and roared:

'I'm going to rip your knickers off you dirty slut.'

His trousers fell to the floor as he came around the

desk, his dick quivering as he went into another bear roar.

Linda looked at him with raised eyebrows, almost disbelieving how well he got into the part. And how the hell were his trousers already undone? Dirty perv must have been fiddling behind his desk. But then he was looming over her and she had to act quickly, turning on her heel and running out of the office, down the stairs and out of the school.

Colin was waiting on the corner, in case anything had gone wrong. They quickly ducked down into Tottenham Court Road tube station, Linda letting Colin get to the escalator step in front of her so they could kiss at the same height.

At home, Linda decanted the Chinese takeout, lounged on the sofa and switched on the TV. Colin edited the video, so that the early section of Linda setting up the seduction was deleted. All that was left was Stephen pretending to be a bear, ready to sexually harass his receptionist, his prick waving about as he beat his chest. Colin automatically recoiling and wanting to look away, hoping it was all worth it.

Obviously Linda didn't show her face the next morning. In the evening, when everyone had left the language school, Colin went in. Stephen looked up, more than disgruntled by the sudden disappearance of his receptionist the previous night and non-appearance of her that morning; and gruffly said:

'Classes have finished for the day.'

'I'm not here for the classes.'

'Well I don't need any more teachers.'

'I'm not here for a job either.'

'Well, what are you bloody here for?'

Colin smiled as he took out the mobile phone, slid it across the desk, and said:

'Press "play".'

Colin and Linda celebrated their second successful scam by lounging on a red leather sofa in the SofaLounge on Lavender Hill, Clapham. Linda was dressed up, a silver feather boa, green one-piece dress, black boots, all recently purchased from designer shops in Covent Garden - a further step up from Top Girl and French Connection. Colin was in his usual jeans and hoody top. Linda scolded him:

'Do you have to always wear the same old top?'

'It's not the same, I bought a new one.'

'Well it might as well be the same. You could have dressed up for the occasion.'

'I'll leave that to you. Don't know how you aren't cold anyway, it's freezing out.'

'Ah you know, us Northern girls, can take a bit of cold unlike you soft Southerners. Cheers.'

Linda raised her glass of champagne:

'Better than cans of Asai beer eh?'

Colin shrugged as he remembered with fondness when they'd first said "cheers" in Japanese. Linda was instantly bubbly after her first sip:

'You know what I'm going to do with the money?'

'What?'

'Get bigger boobs.'

Colin looked askance:

'Really?'

'What's the matter? Thought you'd be happy.'

'What do you mean?'

'You're a breast man.'

Colin cocked his head at her:

'Don't you know anything about me?'

'Don't know why you don't just admit it.'

'Look, if I liked big breasts I wouldn't be with you would I?'

Linda looked at Colin, unsure if it was a compliment or an insult. Feeling light headed after the first glass of bubbly, she shrugged it off:

'What would you have done if you could?'

'I wouldn't have anything done.'

'Not even your bald patch?'

Colin grinned:

'It's not a bald patch.'

'It's getting thinner.'

Colin involuntarily put a hand up to his head:

'Is it?'

'See, touched a sensitive area. Just think, you could

have a hair transplant.'

A meal and two bottles of champagne later, they were back in the flat. Linda took off her dress and stood alluringly in the bedroom doorway with just a feather boa on. Colin didn't waste any time.

CHAPTER 5

Colin and Linda did the same scam each time. If the office was small scale and the boss likely to fall for her charms, Linda would go for the job.

Colin checked where the boss lived, that he had family he would be embarrassed being shown up to, that he had spare money available in his accounts. When he was sure it could work, he let Linda get to work.

She did the same act, seduce and recoil, whether or not the boss or her instigated it, all caught on a hidden iPhone movie. Colin then edited the film, showing Linda to be innocent while her boss was sexually harassing her.

The next day, Colin went in to see the boss, showed the movie clip, laid out the deal – a year's salary or a sexual harassment court case.

Each scam took about a month in total getting the right job, research on the boss, carrying out the seduction and blackmail. Of course it wasn't without its risks. Linda was putting herself in a vulnerable situation. If she didn't get out in time, it could turn nasty, which is why Colin was always nearby on the night of the seduction.

Martin ran an agency finding hotels for foreign tourists in Piccadilly, affording him a nice life with wife and kids in Muswell Hill, the family cosy in their bay windowed three floor red-brick house with garden. In his late forties, Martin was straight as a lace, but positively drooled at the thought of anything extra matrimonial.

As Colin found out, at weekends Martin was the perfect father and husband, taking the kids to swimming lessons in Crouch End and the wife out for a meal in La Chez Maison. But sitting in the pool café, Colin observed Martin's instant delve to his iPhone once the kids were out of sight. And from the restaurant bar he witnessed how Martin clocked younger prettier women a second after his wife went to the toilet.

As Linda discovered, Martin had an internet porn addiction. Going into his office unannounced she caught him quickly hitting keys to get rid of a website. And when he was busy with a client one time, she sneaked in and went through his website search history.

Problem was that Martin wasn't used to attractive young women trying to seduce him and it went to his head, managing to lock the door behind Linda and trying to manhandle her. She was normally alert, but hadn't suspected Martin had it in him. She tried to turn on her heels but got them caught in the carpet, allowing Martin to grab a feel of her buttocks. And now he was nuzzling between her breasts, Linda struggling to protect the bloody iPhone and get her knee free to aim a shot between his legs. But Martin was dry humping her legs so that she was trapped against the wall.

Colin kicked the door in, lock splintering as half the frame came away. Martin so intent on getting inside Linda's bra, he didn't have time to turn around at the noise. Colin instantly grabbed Martin by the shoulders, swung him off Linda and slammed him into the wall, which he slid awkwardly down.

His mouth bleeding, Martin tried to sit up, only for Colin to thud into him, a knee in his chest, pinning his arms down. Martin bucked furiously, until Colin backhanded him across the face, blood smearing across his cheek. Only then Martin submitting as he went into wimp mode.

While Linda adjusted herself, putting her skirt down over her hips as she said to Colin:

'What kept you?'

Martin looked bewildered as he ping-ponged scared glances between Colin and Linda. She stood her heel into his shoulder and twisted:

'You pig.'

Martin squealed in pain before pleading:

'What's going on? I don't understand, you came on to me.' He squirmed to look at Colin:

'Are you the boyfriend? I didn't know, I swear. It's just a misunderstanding. I'm really very sorry. We can clear this up can't we?'

'I think you owe her something.'

'Again, I'm so sorry if I got the wrong impression...'

'I mean you owe her money, not an apology.'

'Money?'

'A year's salary for the job she no longer has.'

'But she does still have a job.'

'She can hardly carry on working for you now can she,

with a boss who sexually harasses her.'

'It won't happen again. We'll arrange a bonus, make everybody happy.'

'A bonus isn't good enough. A year's salary is the deal.'

Martin was starting to come out of his fear and sense that something wrong was going on:

'But wait a minute...what's going on? How did you know she was...'

He wasn't getting it and Colin was getting impatient. Linda was even more impatient, interrupting and holding up the iPhone, containing the video she had quickly been editing:

'Look, let's make this clear. I've got your wife's number. All I need to do is press "send" and within a few seconds she'll get this video of you trying to rape your receptionist. So either you pay or it gets sent.'

'But...'

'One...two...'

'Okay, okay.'

Martin gave in, Colin letting go of him so he could transfer the money while Linda watched.

Each time they took a year's salary, sometimes a little more. After several hits, they had close to two hundred thousand in their joint bank account. There'd also been a couple of misses. One time, the guy had a stroke before Colin had finished his pitch and he'd had to get out quick, Linda complaining that Colin could at least have got the guy to pay before he choked it. Colin learnt to check the guys' health records.

Another guy suddenly broke down and started sobbing. His wife had been having an affair for years herself and he owed money to some bad people. Not wanting any comeback, Colin had let it go. A couple more hits and they'd have around about quarter of a million.

Until then, they splashed out on items they wanted. Colin going for a new flat-screen HD TV, stocking up on DVDs of all the films he loved. He bought both versions of The Postman Always Rings Twice. The remake more explicit, but the original black and white film doing more than enough to stir your imagination, from the moment Lana Turner's lipstick rolled across the floor.

His years abroad meant he was out of touch with recent films, so he harked back to those he'd loved in his teens, creating odd little double bills for himself. Steve McQueen had been the nearest he had to a hero. The Great Escape was Christmas cliché, but you still couldn't beat it when he tried jumping over the fence on his bike. To go with this, Colin bought The Getaway – this time McQueen getting the girl and the money as he escaped to mythical Mexico.

This gave Colin an idea to pair up Butch Cassidy and the Sundance Kid with The Wild Bunch. As a kid he'd loved the former and flinched when he'd seen the latter. But on re-watching, Colin found Butch and Sundance too much of a sentimental parody, whereas the Wild

Bunch was violently brilliant. In both films, crossing over into Mexico didn't end well, but Colin felt that the freeze frame before Redford and Newman got shot to bits was a bit of a cop out compared to Peckinpah's bloodsplattered finale.

The thought crossed Colin's mind that there was something symbolic about him avoiding modern cinema and harking back to his youth. Was he trying to maintain the crime and romance dynamic that tied him and Linda together?

He even bought True Romance for Linda so that they could sit and watch films together. But she was too busy out on clothes shopping sprees, Colin seeing the designer names on bags when they met up in the evening, usually a single name like Anna or Browns, but occasionally extending to first and surname as in Nicole Farhi.

Linda arranged for them to meet in various hotels, phoning from the room she'd booked into. By the time Colin arrived, Linda had done her day's shopping and had had a facial, a massage or her hair done. Applying her lipstick, Linda would point Colin to a shirt she'd purchased and hung up for him. Colin required to be at least smart-casual for drinks and dining.

The first hotel she called from was The Hilton on Park Lane, Linda sexy and seductive as she set up a role-play to meet in the bar as if strangers. On the twenty eighth floor overlooking Hyde Park in one direction and The City in the other, Colin found Linda sipping a cocktail.

Memories of the first time they'd met, their wedding night in Vegas and honeymoon in Cancun flooded in as Colin happily asked if the seat next to her was taken.

The place was supposed to be frequented by European glitterati, whatever that meant. Rich Russians by the look of it. But Colin was ready to go along with Linda's fun, ordering the chef's specialty of lobster tail with artichokes artfully designed around it. More white plate than actual food, but Colin not minding as they got quickly drunk, soon after heading to bed and light-headed sex.

The next hotel didn't give Colin such a buzz. Sat among money-flaunting Italian tourists, the upper-class English setting of The Ritz on Piccadilly reminded Colin of his grandfather's manor house. Still willing to play the game, Colin went for the guinea fowl, which turned out to be more about minimalist design than amount of meat. When Colin thought of traditional British food, it was a plateful of roast dinner. Poking at her duck salad, Linda was more interested in trying different vintage champagnes at thirty pounds a pop. For a working class Northern girl, she was sure developing expensive tastes. Colin had enjoyed it at first, but was bored of the opulence, wanting to get back and watch his old films.

Engrossed in one of his double bills, Colin arrived late at the Savoy on The Strand, Linda already half in the bag from several cocktails, semi-flirting with wealthy Americans. Hungry, Colin went for charcoal grilled chateaubriand, which was basically beef. But at least you got enough to eat. By the time Colin finished, Linda was drunk and fell asleep as soon as they got to their room. As Colin lay there, unable to sleep, he wondered if Linda did the hotel nights to re-live how they'd met or maybe just to avoid going back to the flat.

On the nights back in Tooting, Linda was always despondent as she slouched on the sofa watching TV rather than any of the DVDs Colin had bought. As the place was rented furnished, they couldn't even spend the money getting more comfortable furniture. Linda couldn't see why they still had to be there:

'Why don't we just spend the money and get somewhere nice to live?'

'It will look suspicious if two people who don't have jobs start buying property. Besides, it's not as if we are millionaires is it, we need to do a fair few more hits before we can go and retire somewhere.'

'And where's that going to be?'

'I don't know, how about Thailand?'

'Why Thailand?'

'We can buy a nice place cheap. You can lie on the beach. I can…'

'You can what?'

'I don't know, I'll do something.'

'You wouldn't know what to do. You hate beaches, you need to do things. You know what I think, I think you love the whole adventure of it, that you don't want to stop.'

Colin thought of retorting, but told himself to be nice:

'Two hundred thousand isn't even going to buy us a flat in London. We're better off saving it up then getting out of here.'

Linda shrugged, turned away from Colin and picked up the remote. Colin didn't like her silence:

'Come on, don't get pouty on me. We'll work something out.'

Staring at the TV as it came on, Linda said:

'You better.'

An empty threat, thought Colin. But maybe she was right, doubts creeping in. He had thought they were playing from the same script, but in reality he wanted the adventure, she just wanted an easy life. They had a good deal going, but could it last?

When it came, the argument didn't take Colin by surprise but the force of Linda's venom did.

Bringing a margarita in from the pizza delivery man at the door, Linda nodded to Colin:

'It's your turn to pay.'

'I didn't know we had turns.'

'Well I paid for the last one and the man's waiting.'

Not wanting to argue in front of someone else, Colin paid off the pizza delivery man.

They sat eating the pizza without speaking, music coming out of the stereo, another of Colin's Stone Roses CDs. Colin knew he shouldn't, but he couldn't help making a comment:

'Just because we've got ourselves a bit of money doesn't mean we have to stop cooking.'

'Why would I cook if I don't have to? If you want to I'm not stopping you.'

'I'm not going to do it all.'

'Then don't.'

Colin didn't further the argument, waiting until Linda made her move, knowing what was coming, the weekly argument about money.

From the start, they'd set up a joint account which the money went into. It had a daily limit of how much could be taken out from cash machines. Any big sums to be taken out required both their signatures. Sure enough, Linda broke the deadlock:

'I'm fed up of sitting in this crappy flat, not using the money. You know, I've been thinking. It's me who puts myself in a risky situation. I could be raped if it goes wrong. So I should get sixty percent.'

'But it all goes into our joint account anyway.'

'That's another thing. We need separate accounts. Then I can spend my money how I want to.'

'We talked about that at the start. It's too complicated for someone to transfer the money into two accounts.'

'We can do it afterwards. We could split what we've got now, sixty into mine, forty into yours, then do the same after each hit.'

'What does it matter, we're married aren't we, sharing everything?'

'But it's not equal sharing; I'm the one doing the dirty work.'

'I'm not doing nothing. I do all the research before and I'm the one who goes in at the end. If we can find a female employer who it will work with, we'll swap roles.'

'Or maybe a gay boss.'

Linda smiled at Colin, but it wasn't natural, it was one of her fake smiles, used for people she didn't give a fuck about. She carried on:

'I don't know what you're doing all day supposedly doing research with your Slovakian au pairs.'

'Hey, you're the one seducing other men, which I've got to watch each time.'

Linda sneered:

'Well what kind of man lets his wife do that?'

Colin couldn't answer that. It had been her idea in the first place, but she was making out as if he made her do it. He should never have agreed to it initially. He didn't think she would actually go with one of the men, but he didn't know what happened when the camera wasn't on.

Colin's silent mulling was interrupted, Linda spitting out:

'And can you turn off this music. How many times do I have to listen to this shit?'

Linda left Colin with the remains of the pizza as she turned from him and turned on the TV. Colin got up and turned off the stereo. He'd bought all the old stuff he used to listen to – Stone Roses, Happy Mondays and

Primal Scream collections. Linda had bought a Madonna hits CD in nostalgia and Amy Winehouse out of female alliance.

Maybe it summed up how different they were. He'd thought they were after the same adventure, but it turned out they were playing to a different tune. The excitement of the scams had briefly brought back the passion, but it had simply become a business venture, a deadly one.

CHAPTER 6

When they looked through the job ads, they did it in silence without any music. When the pizza was delivered at night, Linda watched TV while she ate. Colin shook his head, resigned. The pizza boxes were piling up.

It had gone from less sex and more arguments to none of either. They didn't go out for meals together and they didn't cook, not that Linda could anyway.

With things as they were maybe they didn't concentrate as much as they should have on the next job.

In theory, Nigel seemed like the perfect fall guy. He had a small office in Covent Garden arranging short term lets, aimed at naïve or rich foreigners prepared to pay over the odds for a couple of months. He had a house in Hampstead, with wife and family. He was losing his hair and shape and was desperate for some attractive woman to make him feel young. And he had a couple of easily accessible bank accounts.

Colin was anxious as the only time they ever spoke to each other was to give the necessary information. Linda would look at him with her calm expression, telling him details of Nigel's office and bank accounts. But she wasn't telling him everything.

He'd seen her hand surreptitiously move her hair away from her face, as if it was a natural gesture. What it showed to Colin was that she failed to mention how she'd got the info they needed, playing on her co-worker's desire, a student temp who was head over heels with her.

During his own research, he'd casually visited a bar the guy was in with his university mates. Rupert the guy's name was, just twenty one, and he couldn't stop telling his mates about this hot secretary who'd come on to him. According to Rupert, she'd taken him back to a hotel and ridden him senseless. Colin clenched his fists, his heart pounding as he wanted to wade over and smash his beer glass into Rupert's face, but he told himself it was just bravado by Rupert in front of his mates.

Colin had seen how Rupert waited every night to walk to the tube with Linda, how she left him hanging with a kiss on the cheek each time. She was playing him that was all.

On his part, Colin provided details of Nigel's family life and circumstances, but didn't mention the Czech au pair who was more than eager to divulge information, especially after their third date where they'd kissed. She initiated it, but he hadn't hesitated, enjoying the relief.

Two weeks into the job, Linda was putting on her lipstick one morning when she announced:

'I'm going to do it tonight.'

'Thanks for the notice.'

'Don't worry about it.'

'What time?'

'Seven.'

Linda gave herself a final look in the mirror and left the flat without a "goodbye".

Waiting in an alley across from Nigel's agency, it seemed to Colin that it was taking much longer than usual. He'd received no quickly sent empty text to show that he needed to intervene, but if it carried on for much longer, he would have to go in and check. Humiliating images came into his mind. Maybe Linda was doing it deliberately, actually was fucking Nigel, just so Colin would go in and find them doing it. Nigel was an ugly man, but Linda would no doubt do it, just to humiliate Colin.

Inside the office, Linda was finding it much harder going than usual. Sure, if Nigel could have her he would without a second thought, but he was too realistic a business man and knew that there had to be some catch for a girl like Linda to be after an ugly bastard like himself. He wasn't delusional:

'What are you after Linda, a pay rise?'

Linda crossed her legs, giving him a flash of thigh.

'Well I wouldn't say no.'

'Then why don't you just ask for it?'

'I just thought that I could repay in kind.'

'You have a very hard time coming right out and saying something. Linda, you're an intelligent good-looking woman, what's this all about?'

Linda put her mouth into a suggestive smile. Nigel wasn't easy to manipulate. Maybe she should have waited another week. She paused a moment and unbuttoned her shirt, holding his eyes:

'Are you telling me you don't want to fool around?'

Nigel had his hands behind his head. He was enjoying the scene. Making sure there was no catch:

'So let's look at this. You want a higher salary. And in return, apart from your good work, you're offering what exactly?'

None of the wording was any good, she needed him to say something incriminating. She played for time:

'That depends.'

'On what exactly? Maybe I'm being a bit stupid here – think you could get to the point?'

'Maybe you could suggest some different rates.'

'Different rates hey?'

Nigel smirked, looked at Linda with his little eyes. What a slut, he thought, an opportunity not to be missed. He visualised pushing her over the desk, raising her skirt, hearing her moan as he pushed into her. He put his hand on his crotch, as if to unzip his trousers:

'Ok, you show me yours and I'll show you mine. You wrap those nice lips around my cock and I'll give you a five percent pay rise. You place your sweet pussy on top of it and I'll give you ten.'

Finally, thought Linda, the scumbag reveals himself and at last something on camera that could be used. Relaxing, she raised her eyebrows, as if to say that was not enough. Sure enough, Nigel piped up:

'Ten and I'm not going higher. I think we'll both be getting pleasure out of this.'

Linda's fake smile instantly turned into a sneer:

'I don't think so. That's what I need in my life right now, a sweaty pig like you?'

Without further ado, she turned, leaving the office, not seeing Nigel squint after her.

Colin saw her leave and caught up with her as she headed for the tube:

'Everything alright?'

'Why wouldn't it be?'

That was as far as their conversation went. Linda two steps ahead on the escalators down to the underground, Colin not bothering to reach her the escalator kiss ritual long since dissolved. They sat in silence as the tube rattled off. Linda was in fact uneasy. Every other time, there had been a more dramatic rebuff, the man either swearing at her back or physically trying to manhandle her. Nigel had just taken it. It didn't bode well, but she decided not to say anything to Colin. The amount of time she'd been in there, she could have been raped for all he knew, but did he care?

For his part, Colin was also uneasy. When he'd arrived in Covent Garden to go and wait in the alley, an Italian couple had asked if he could take their photo. He had done so, no problem, but then began to wish he hadn't. If it ever came to something, two witnesses who could place him at the location. It was unlikely, but he didn't like it. Not that he would dream of telling Linda.

The next day, Colin went to Nigel's office. He was about to walk straight in when he saw through the glass door, the student temp still at his desk, so backtracked, waited in one of the cafes, fiddling with a coffee cup. Half hour later, the temp left and Colin went in.

From the back office, Nigel shouted out:

'We're closed.'

Colin continued on into Nigel's office. Nigel looked up from his computer with disbelief on his face:

'Are you deaf? I said we're closed.'

'No I'm not deaf and I guess you're not blind.'

'What's that supposed to mean?'

'It means you should look at this.'

Colin placed the mobile phone on Nigel's desk. Nigel looked down at the phone then back up at Colin:

'And why should I do that?'

'Because the video shows you sexually harassing my wife.'

A slight smile appeared on Nigel's face. He picked up the phone, pressed "play" and watched the edited video, containing only the part with him offering a pay rise in return for a blow job and sex. When the video finished, Nigel put the phone back on the desk and looked straight at Colin, saying:

'And your point is?'

'Pay us her year's salary and we won't take you to court on sexual harassment charges. We're reasonable people. Your wife, kids, nobody needs to know about this. Pay us and you don't have to worry about us.'

Nigel began to nod, then laughed:

'Do I look worried? Okay, take me to court.'

That wasn't what Colin had been expecting. He didn't like how the situation was developing one bit. Nigel leaned forward:

'In fact if you don't take me to court, I'll take you. You don't understand shit, do you? You see that?'

Nigel pointed to a top corner of the room. Colin followed Nigel's fat finger, looking up to see a tiny CCTV camera installed. Nigel went on:

'I've got all of last night on tape, which will show the little act your wife put on before trying to frame me. She's smoking hot, I'll give you that. I've also got you on tape trying to extort money from me.'

Nigel gave a courtly wave to the camera:

'Smile.'

Colin didn't smile, but Nigel did:

'Cat got your tongue?'

Colin looked around for something to hit Nigel with. He knew he should stay calm, but the way Nigel was sitting there relaxed, squeezed into his wide-boy suit was driving Colin mad. Maybe he should just reach over and smash Nigel's head down onto the desk a few times. It would make him feel better, but it wouldn't solve the problem, and it wouldn't be too clever having it on tape. He bit down his anger and tried to bluff:

'I guess we can call it quits as you did still try to get

Linda to suck you.'

Colin stumbled a little as he threw his last dice:

'I'm sure you wouldn't want your wife and kids knowing about it.'

Nigel didn't seem to care:

'See you in court. Now fuck off out of my office.'

Colin glanced up at the camera as he slowly rose. For the first time, Colin knew how the men they'd set up felt. If he'd had a tail, it would have been between his legs.

Back at the flat, Colin had no choice but to tell Linda what had happened. He tried telling it over a cup of tea, making it appear not such a big deal:

'Maybe he's just bluffing.'

'Maybe he wants me to go back working there as well, as if nothing happened.'

In case Colin hadn't got her sarcasm, Linda made it clear:

'Or maybe he wants me to suck his fat cock. Thought about that?'

Colin tried to remain optimistic, figure a way to turn the situation around. But nothing much came to mind:

'Anyway, he doesn't have our address does he – you gave a false one didn't you?'

'What do you think? Of course I did. It doesn't stop him trying to find it though does it. You've really fucked it up big time haven't you.'

'I fucked it up?'

'Yes, you Brains. You're the one who's supposed to do all the research, check that he won't want his family to know.'

'You're the one in the office all day. Was it asking too much for you to take a proper look around? Maybe then you might have noticed there was a bloody camera in the ceiling.'

'Just like you didn't see it until he pointed it out.'

'Just like you didn't tell me about the other bloke who worked there, sitting there just as I was about to go in. I had to wait until he left.'

'He wasn't important. He should have already left. You probably got there to early.'

'I didn't get there too early. Maybe you didn't mention him because he's young and handsome and you've been fucking him to get information.'

'Just like you and your au pair I expect. You didn't mention one, but I'll bet there was, some Eastern European girl with big tits was it?'

'Anything's better than nothing.'

Linda lashed out, slapping Colin hard across the face and leaving an angry red hand print. He swung the cup in his hand, abruptly halted halfway, instead throwing it against the wall, the cup smashing. Colin turned back to Linda, breathing hard. She didn't flinch:

'What are you going to do, beat me up? You're no different from those cowardly slobs. You haven't got the guts.'

As always she had to have the last word. The two of them stared each other out in a standoff. Colin's hand had curled into a fist. Linda's lips were curled in hate. Colin no longer wanted to kiss them, he wanted to hit them.

CHAPTER 7

A week later, a letter from Nigel's solicitor dropped through the door.

He hadn't been bluffing and he had found out their address. It probably hadn't been that difficult. Linda hadn't lied about her surname. They were registered for council tax and other bills. A solicitor would find ways of obtaining it.

The letter stated that the solicitor's client Nigel Hall was taking Colin Crosswell and Linda Collins to court for attempted blackmail. Colin passed the letter over to Linda:

'We better get our own solicitors.'

Linda didn't reply, just sighed as she took out a business card from her handbag, and tossed it towards Colin. He picked it up off the floor, Bromwood and Partners, Solicitors in Holborn. Seeing she was one step ahead, Colin said:

'Phone then will I?'

'Think that would be a good idea wouldn't it.'

It was the first reply she'd given all week, delivered with full sarcasm and no eye contact.

Hugh, the solicitor taking their case, had an upside down face, shaved head with a goatee beard. Sat across from them in his office in Vernon Place, Holborn, big windows overlooking the walkway of coffee shops below, he was wearing an expensive blue suit. Linda was dressed up in a sophisticated manner, almost for work, in formal skirt that ended a few inches above her knees and a shirt that showed her figure. Colin was in his usual jeans and hoody top.

Linda smiled when she was telling the story or being talked to by Hugh, brushing her hair aside with that flirty way she had. As soon as Colin talked, her mouth fell into a silent sneer.

Hugh listened to both of them individually, his hands together, pointing up, tips of his fingers touching his goatee and stroking it thoughtfully, head turning when it was the others turn to speak. When both of them had nothing else to add, Hugh smiled:

'It is a difficult case, no two ways about it. But, we'll find a solution. What we need to do here is twofold. First, we can set up the option to plead extenuating circumstances, that is you were driven to do what you did by desperation. You'd recently lost your job, been abused by your previous boss etc.

'Second, we need to start digging into his past and see what we can find. He doesn't sound like Mr. Innocent himself. Quite possibly we can find something he doesn't want brought up in court and we can then use that as leverage to conclude an amicable deal with him.'

Having spent the previous six months doing his own bluffing, Colin knew Hugh was all talk, but he wanted to believe him.

Hugh stood up, put his hand out:

'I'll be in touch.'

Linda took Hugh's hand, giving him her best smile. Colin gave a perfunctory handshake.

Outside, Linda didn't tell Colin where she was going or even say "goodbye", simply walked off, presumably to go clothes shopping in Covent Garden. Colin didn't know what to do with himself.

He walked vacantly, like the ghost of a tourist. Down through business-minded Holborn and tourist-covered Covent Garden, past taxi-lined Charing Cross and tube-exiting Embankment, over the pedestrian packed bridge, tourists stopping to take photos of the view. On the South Bank, he simply leant against the low wall, staring into the Thames, lost in thought. How had it all unravelled so fast? Was there any way they could get through this and still be together?

Obviously they couldn't pull any more scams. And he didn't feel like doing any old job. There was money in the bank, but unless they both agreed to split it, it would stay there. Linda was holding out for sixty percent. He didn't see why he should accept that, he'd put in as much work as her, probably more with all his snooping. Besides, he was pretty sure that if he caved in on sixty percent, she'd soon chisel away for more. His share down to twenty, then ten, then nothing. Without both their signatures the money was staying put, so until they could figure a way out of the situation, he wasn't giving in.

Living in the flat together was intolerable. They didn't speak or sleep together. One night, Linda had plonked the spare duvet on the sofa, said one of her occasional sentences:

'I don't see why I should move out of the bed, so you can sleep here.'

There was no response to that. It would have been too humiliating to beg to be let back in. And what was the point. They'd long stopped having sex. For over a month now it had been no touching, faces to the wall, backs to each other.

Another time, she was sitting on the sofa, watching TV, when she idly took off her wedding ring and without looking, dropped it into the empty pizza box, among the crusts.

Turning to go somewhere, he didn't know where, Colin noticed the posters outside the National Film Theatre. A season of Nicholas Ray films. He didn't know who Nicholas Ray was, but he did know a few of the other names.

James Dean in Rebel Without a Cause – just what Colin felt like. Humphrey Bogart In a Lonely Place – and that was just where Colin was.

Colin went on in, checked the times showing. The first film of the day was on in twenty minutes time – They Live by Night. Why not, thought Colin, he had nothing else to do.

The last time Colin had been to the cinema was almost

a year earlier, in Japan, with Linda. He sat back, ready to forget. His eyes adjusted first to the dark of the cinema then to the black and white film that came on.

A two-shot close-up of a young man and woman's face, with the caption:

"This boy and this girl were never properly introduced into the world we live in."

And then a helicopter shot of a getaway car, speeding away…

For just over an hour and a half, Colin lost himself in the doomed romance, the attempted escape to freedom, the menacing world of crime there was no way out of…

Colin stumbled out of the cinema, out into the real world, clasped the wall once more, not taking in the Thames below, his mind still with the film.

Maybe everything was going to be alright. Sure the ending wasn't too happy, but she'd stuck with him throughout it all. And then it dawned on him. It was nothing like him and Linda.

There were no similarities with the film whatsoever. Linda was filled with hate towards him and he was full of resentment towards her. The film had given him a brief respite, a belief that everything would turn out ok. The light of day revealed a different picture.

It was late when Colin finally made it back to the flat. The lights were all off. Linda wasn't back yet. He sat watching TV until he fell asleep on the sofa.

At some point in the early hours of the morning Colin heard the front door opening. Linda drunkenly bumping into things as she entered the flat. Colin froze as he heard her giggly whisper:

'Oops I bumped into something.'

Immediately Colin thought he knew what she was doing. Bringing another man back to the flat, her ultimate way of humiliating him. But as she passed through the living room, he saw she was talking into her mobile phone. She didn't spare a look for Colin on the sofa, but went straight into the bedroom, her bedroom now as she drunkenly slammed the door behind her.

Colin couldn't hear what she was saying, just the occasional giggle. He thought about standing outside the bedroom door to listen in, but instead shivered as he walked away, remembering hearing his dad have drunken sex with the local barmaid all those years ago, the same sense of shame flooding through him. Eventually, the giggling stopped but Colin still couldn't get to sleep, spending the next few hours staring up at the ceiling.

The next morning, Colin got up, making himself a cup of tea. The flat was a mess, full of empty pizza boxes and unwashed cups. But only half were his, Linda's wedding ring still lying among the debris. They ordered their meals separately and made their own cups of tea, so he was fucked if he was cleaning her stuff up. He washed his cups and took out his half of the pizza boxes, putting them in one of the big metal bins outside. He paused, pulled off his wedding ring and chucked it in the metal bin.

He still didn't know what to do with himself. He walked around the streets of Tooting, past the terraced houses and corner shops, and was still none the wiser, apart from further confirming that they didn't live in Chelsea or South Ken for sure. Full of self pity, he promised himself that if he ever got out of this mess he'd change, get a regular job and steady girlfriend and never fuck up again. He went back to the flat.

Linda had got up, steam from the shower lingering with newly sprayed perfume. Colin went into the kitchen, putting the kettle on to make a coffee. As she passed through the living room, Linda checked the time and saw it was quarter to ten already. How did time go so quickly? Without a glance at Colin, Linda walked on past, jacket on, and out of the flat.

On instinct, Colin left his coffee unfinished, following after Linda. As expected, she was headed towards the tube station. Following her was going to be harder than with the bosses. He could be sitting next to them and they wouldn't know who he was. Not much chance of that with Linda.

He held back as much as possible before going into the station and getting onto the tube, in a different carriage.

At Tottenham Court Road, he saw her get off and change onto the Central Line, eastbound. He was pretty sure he could guess where she was going.

Sure enough, Linda got off at Holborn. Knowing she would head towards the solicitors, Colin kept his distance. But Linda didn't go into the building housing Hugh's office, turning instead into one of the cafes in the street below.

Hugh got up when Linda arrived, kissing her on both cheeks. She sat and coffee was ordered. Hugh said something and Linda's mouth opened in seductive laughter, her hand on his arm. Colin caught all of it on his mobile phone video camera. He didn't know what they were plotting, but it might come in useful to have it on camera.

Colin left them to it, walking away with his phone in his hand, holding it tight. His and Linda's marriage had ended. So had their business venture. They were no longer partners in any sense. It was simply about the money now – who would and wouldn't get it.

CHAPTER 8

On the day of the court hearing, Linda wore her silk green dress he'd first seen her in as a hostess in Tokyo. It was a strange choice seeing the wardrobe she had available, but it was damn sexy, Colin had to admit.

For a second he felt something for her again, wanted her, just as it had been at the start. Maybe that was also why she had worn it. But on catching Linda casting a sideways sneer at him, Colin snapped out of it. For whatever reason she was wearing the dress, it wasn't for him.

Colin had at least shaved and swapped his hoody for a more formal jacket. They had to appear as if they were innocent people, driven to do what they did by despair. And they were to remain silent until called to speak by either Hugh or the judge.

The two of them sat silently side by side in the dock. Behind the plastic panel, it felt as if they were already halfway to prison. Hugh had promised nothing like that would happen, but Colin still felt the sweat dripping down his arms.

The court was empty apart from the clerk, prosecuting and defence counsel. Colin hoped he would remain calm when Nigel, the smarmy bastard, entered - refraining from leaping out of the dock and throttling him. Hugh suddenly appeared by their side, whispering excitedly:

'Good news people. We've got what we needed. He's

been in court before for keeping cameras in places he shouldn't, women's toilets!'

Just then the judge, complete with wig and gown, swished in from the back of the court. Hugh quickly sat to the side in the spectators' gallery. The clerk called out:

'All rise.'

All five present rose. Linda was looking directly at the judge, a flicker of a smile tugging at her mouth as she studied him.

Colin followed her gaze. He was fairly young for a judge, forties perhaps, the wig of grey curls made it hard to guess his age. He also had a curly beard and moustache. Not unhandsome, but anyone hiding behind all that hair, real or fake, had to have something to hide.

The prosecuting counsel had gone up to the judge and was furtively explaining something in a low voice. The defence counsel was relaxed as he waited.

The prosecution went sheepishly back to his place. The judge sighed, speaking as if there was a bigger audience than there was:

'It would appear that the prosecution witness and claimant has failed to turn up, and in fact is unlikely to turn up in the future due to new evidence being brought to light. The case is therefore dismissed and any complaint against the defendants waived, both now and at any future date. Court dismissed.'

Without further ado, the judge turned and swished out the door at the back of the court. The prosecution sheepishly packed his papers. The defence turned to Hugh and shrugged. Colin and Linda both sighed in relief, for a brief second in unison.

After all the anxiety, that was it, case dismissed in a few minutes. It had been a bluff by Nigel all along, he never was going to actually get himself shown up in court, he just wanted to string them along. And he had been spying on women in toilets. Any reunion Colin imagined was swiftly crushed as Linda turned to him:

'You have five days to pay me what I earned.'

She handed Colin a scrap of paper. He looked at it without comprehension:

'What's this?'

'My new bank account. You just have to come in and sign with me that seventy percent of our joint account goes into it.'

'Seventy?'

'Yep, seventy. Got a problem with that? Thirty of something is a lot better than nothing.'

'What if I don't sign?'

Linda let that hang, then sighed and shrugged:

'Well, there's different ways. You really want to play games?'

Linda left him with that to think about as she waltzed out of the defence box. Outside the courtroom, Linda was gushing in her thanks to Hugh:

'Thanks for everything Hugh. You've been wonderful.'

'See, told you we'd sort it out didn't I.'

Linda gave him one of her best smiles, kissed him on the cheek. Turning, she ignored Colin as she brushed past him, on her way out of the court buildings.

Colin and Hugh simply shook hands.

Hugh then went into the toilets. Colin followed him in. While Hugh was pissing into the urinal, Colin stood by the side, folding a piece of paper in his hands. Colin said:

'Hugh, what were you and Linda meeting about?'

'Sorry?'

'Don't play the innocent. I know you two had secret meetings without me.'

'They weren't secret.'

'I want to know what she is trying to do.'

'Confidential I'm afraid.'

'She's my wife.'

'And she's my client.'

'So am I.'

'But she is also my separate client.'

'Do you have coffee with all your clients?'

'There's no rule against it.'

'But I'm sure your employer wouldn't be happy to see video evidence of your client kissing you.'

It was pathetic, but Colin was desperate. Hugh finished and did himself up:

'Colin, it's no secret that I don't go for women, so whatever scheme you're planning, forget it.'

The anger and frustration burst out of Colin. Without

warning, he smashed his forehead into Hugh's face. Blood burst out of Hugh's nose.

Hugh staggered back, holding his blood-flowing nose. Colin pulled him up by his shirt collar, an agonised moan escaping from Hugh's throat as Colin got a tight grip on his suit waist, trousers digging into his scrotum.

'You want to talk about client confidentiality,' Colin walking Hugh to the toilet cubicle, 'you want to tell me about it?'

Colin ran Hugh toward the toilet, kicked his legs from under him and shoved his head down into the soiled water sloshing around the bowl.

Colin had never been that violent in his life, but adrenalin was pumping through him, rage dictating his actions.

'Ok, how about you tell me how she's trying to do me over.'

Hugh pleaded from the edge of the toilet, spitting out pieces of wet paper and spluttering:

'Come on Colin, please don't do this.'

Colin started to force Hugh's head down into the toilet. Hugh's high-pitched voice came up:

'Ok, I'll talk.'

Colin lifted Hugh's head. Hugh gasped:

'If the case was going to go against you she wanted to say that it was your idea, that she was forced to take part because she was afraid of you.'

'But the case went our way.'

'Yes.'

'So what about now?'

Hugh sighed:

'She wanted to see if it's possible to file for divorce on grounds of violence and in a way that you wouldn't be entitled to any of the money.'

Colin let go of Hugh's hair, calm now that he knew Linda's plan. Hugh slumped against the cubicle wall. Colin asked:

'Is that possible?'

'Well after your behaviour just now, probably yes!' Hugh could still joke, Colin admired that.

'But even if she got the divorce, the money would be split evenly.'

'Unless she can find a way to prove that it was originally hers and you took it from her, yes.'

Colin nodded. He looked down at Hugh, took the toilet roll off its hook, dropped the roll onto Hugh's lap, said:

'Here. Sorry about your nose.'

Leaving Hugh to clean himself up, Colin left the toilets and walked out of the courts.

Southwark Crown Courts were next to London Bridge. Colin could simply get on the Northern Line and head back to the flat, but what the hell was waiting for him there. Hell, that was what. The court case was over, just like he and Linda were over. What was left? A joint bank account full of blackmail money that neither could access. A broken dream of the two of them escaping to some exotic beach. He couldn't stand being in the flat with her any more. And if she wasn't there, he would just be wondering what it was she was up to.

He crossed over, down past the Cathedral, under the intersecting rail bridges, onto cobbled streets, the old London dungeon up ahead.

Colin stopped dead.

An old warehouse had been converted into a trendy glass fronted wine bar. And coming out of the wine bar was Linda, her arm interlinked with a man's arm. A man in his forties, with curly dark hair and beard and... without a wig. The judge. She was with the judge.

Colin watched in stunned disbelief as the judge opened the door of a bright yellow remodelled VW beetle, that year's model. He sure liked to be seen. Linda got in, beaming a smile, her hair the same colour as the car. The judge shut Linda's door then went around to the driver's side, almost with a little trot, got in the driver's seat. The car drove off.

Colin didn't know if he was shocked or satisfied. At least he knew who she was with, he just had to find out what she was planning. Jesus she was devious. She'd had two plans going simultaneously in case things didn't go their way. With Hugh, she'd planned to make it look as if it was all Colin's doing. With the judge, Colin could only guess it was to make him give a ruling their way.

Colin was so shocked, he hadn't noticed the woman

that had been standing next to him for a good few minutes, been there since before the car drove off. Until he heard her say in a strong South American accent that he immediately placed as Brazilian:

'You the husband huh?'

CHAPTER 9

Colin turned to look at the woman standing next to him. She was still looking to where the yellow VW had turned out of sight, staring out of dark sunglasses, big round ones. The sun was out, thought Colin, but it wasn't that bright. It was only April.

From her light brown skin, Colin was now sure she was Brazilian mulatto like half the population there. The woman's colour and accent hitting Colin with a sudden flashback to his time on the cruise ships. In particular, Maria, the Brazilian waitress he'd fallen for. The prettiest girl on board without doubt, she'd rebuffed all advances but loved hanging out with Colin – telling him about the joy of the carnivals and poverty of the favelas. One night, with the full moon lighting up the sea, they'd kissed. But Maria had danced off to bed alone, saying she didn't want to start a relationship on the ship. Strangely this didn't stop her fucking Vinnie senseless for the next few months – one of the reasons why Colin docked in Japan.

The woman standing next to him on the streets of London wasn't anywhere near as beautiful as Maria, but not bad looking. Her face told him she was in her late twenties, maybe a bit older, but not much. A bit of meat on her, most of it on her breasts, Colin's eyes making their way down. The woman really had the most amazing breasts. You could only see the top curves, but it was enough to show that they were huge, round and brown, her nipples pointing right at him through her top. Colin grinned:

'Do I know you?'

The woman looked at him:

'Not yet you don't know me.'

She wore a skimpy skirt that barely covered her behind and her breasts were tightly placed under a garishly coloured flower print stretch-to-fit top. Maybe that was what she needed the sunglasses for, thought Colin, her own top. He managed to drag his eyes away from her chest:

'Well, nice talking to you. See you around.'

But just as he was about to turn away, she repeated herself, her broken and heavily accented English loud and not so clear:

'You no hear? I say are you the husband?'

Colin turned back:

'What it's got to do with you?'

'You don't see a problem they are fodendo?'

'Eh?'

'They are fodendo, they are fucking.'

'I guessed that. Like I said, what I don't understand is what it's got to do with you.'

'I have something to show you.'

Colin knew what it was he wanted her to show him:

'What exactly is it you want to show me?'

'You have a DVD player?'

Colin checked his pockets:

'Not on me. Guess I must have left it at home.'

'You go there now?'

'That's where I'm heading. It's been one hell of a morning.'

'Good, we go there then. Which way, London Bridge?'

She started walking in that direction. Colin stood watching her walk away. She stopped and looked back:

'You just going to stand looking at my arse and holding your testiclos or we going to get down to business?'

Colin tried to grasp the situation:

'Sorry, but who are you?'

'Who am I? I'm the answer to all your problems. My name is Barbara de Santos.'

Colin wanted to get it straight in his mind:

'Is this a sex thing?'

'Please…we going to talk business, about judge and your wife. Look, you buy me coffee, I explain. Then we go to your place, watch DVD. You find interesting, I think.'

Colin shrugged in agreement. With the case out of the way, he had nothing better to do.

They walked through to the walkway by the Thames, sat at a coffee place, inset from the riverside. Barbara ordered a latte, lit up a Silk Cut, raised her sunglasses onto her dark hair. She had blue eyes, shining out of her coffee-coloured skin. A definite mulatto thought Colin. He wished he smoked, just to have something in his hands.

Cigarette in one hand, latte in the other, Barbara looked at Colin:

'One year ago, I come from Brazil, get a job as a cleaner. I think you guess who for, Mr. Stephenson.'

'Who?'

'Judge Stephenson, the man who is fodendo your wife.'

Colin smiled thinly, this time getting Barbara's use of Brazilian:

'Thanks for letting the whole world know.'

'Don't you worry, the whole world will know when I finish with them. You see I am his cleaner but I also become his lover. He buy me all sorts of nice things, clothes, mobile…'

Barbara pulled at her brightly coloured top and held up her mobile, making it clear what she was talking about. She inhaled on her cigarette before continuing:

'Not only this, he promise me many things. Most important he promise to sort out my visa. Then few weeks ago, she come along.'

Barbara spat a little coffee on the ground before she resumed:

'Now I am no longer lover, no longer important. Not being his lover I don't mind so much, but the promise of visa…'

Barbara paused to have a drag of her cigarette and slurp of her coffee. Colin used the pause to get his breath back from listening to her.

'You know when my visa run out? Today. Does he care? No, he lost in his sexy little world with your whore wife. Is her fault. Why I need revenge on the both of them. I think maybe this interests you, no?'

Colin didn't immediately realise he was being asked a question. Barbara looked at him:

'You a bit slow? You happy that your wife sleep with another man?"

'I don't care what she does anymore, but I do have my own reasons for getting back at her.'

'Ok, so we work together.'

'How did you know she's my wife?'

'Was cleaning, found a note that the judge was looking at her court case today. So came on down, saw the two of you go in.'

'Jesus, everyone is following everyone.'

'You don't have to tell me what was about.'

'Hey, that's very kind of you.'

'To do with last boss hey?'

'Thought I didn't have to tell you.'

'Just if you want.'

Colin almost laughed. He was sitting talking with a Brazilian woman he had never met before who had a stupendous bosom and didn't care what she said. He shrugged:

'Her last boss was trying to sue us for attempted blackmail. I guess fucking your judge was her back-up plan, in case the case went wrong.'

'Did it?'

'No.'

'So why she still fucking him?'

'I don't know, but she'll have her reasons.'

'Well however you planning to get back at her, you need me, I got keys to the judge's place, can get inside, know him and the house inside out.'

Colin didn't know what he wanted. He knew Linda was planning something so that she could have all the money. There would be no negotiating, it was all or nothing. So he had to be one up, have something on her. He asked:

'Okay so you say you can help me, but what do you get out of it?'

'Now, I am alone. Is always good to have a man by your side. I help you. In return you help me.'

'How exactly?'

Barbara patted her handbag:

'First we watch movie, then we discuss plan.'

'What kind of "movie"?'

'Home movie.'

'Which kind of home movie?'

Colin cautious as it was home movies that had created this mess in the first place.

'You watch, you see.'

Colin looked at Barbara. She was quite possibly mad and it took a lot to understand her. She said everything directly and didn't get sarcasm. But she could be useful and what was there to lose by seeing whatever it was she had to show.

'Ok, come on, let's go back to mine.'

Barbara took a final drag of her cigarette and stubbed it out, downed the last of her coffee, dropped her sunglasses back in place, lifted her handbag over her shoulder and stood up ready to go.

Getting off at Tooting Broadway tube station, Barbara stopped and looked around, eyebrows raised almost to the sunglasses on her head:

'Where is this, end of the world?'

'No, just the end of the Northern Line, or almost. There's a couple more stops.'

'I think is far enough thank you.'

'Bit rough for you?'

'Pah, is nothing. In Rio, soon as you get in your car, you don't stop. You stop at a traffic light, you get man pointing a gun at you through the window. Three times it happen to me. You go to work, man point gun at your face. Go to shops man point gun at you. Want to report to police? Man point gun at you on the way. This man, he is everywhere – is why I come to London. '

Watching the street life, Colin saw her point – it wasn't that Tooting was rough, just a bit dead.

'Were the guns loaded?'

Barbara stared at Colin:

'How I know if they were loaded? I don't stop and say

excuse me, but can you show me if your gun is loaded so I know to give you my money or not.'

Barbara shook her head. This guy really asked some dumb questions. Taking another look around, Tooting proved what she'd started to realise – London's streets weren't paved with gold. Okay in Rio she hadn't been rich but her secretarial job in the university had a certain amount of respect attached to it, unlike being a cleaner. But more important than anything, Rio had sun and beaches. That's what she missed the most. British weather just made everyone miserable. How did anyone live here for more than a few years? Why was she? Her thoughts were interrupted by Colin:

'So you want to stay and admire the view or you coming?'

Barbara tottered after Colin, down Totterdown Street, her breasts jiggling in time to the clack of her impossibly high heels, Colin almost smiling as he made the connection. He thought about making some joke to Barbara but just knew she wouldn't get it.

Not only was Barbara not impressed with the area Colin lived in, she wasn't too enthralled by the flat either, or more the state it was in. The kitchen was full of dirty cups and plates. Pizza boxes and Chinese takeaway containers were stacked up, remains of crusts and dried rice inside.

'You don't have a cleaner no?'

'Can't get the staff these days.'

Colin was making a joke, but Barbara didn't get it:

'Then why not you?'

'Hey, none of this is mine, it's all stuff Linda leaves. She wouldn't clean mine, so why am I going to clean hers?'

'Is bit childish no?'

'Sorry it's not up to the high standards you're obviously used to.'

'The judge he lives in very nice clean house – in Highgate, see all city from his window. Maybe is reason why your wife like to be there.'

'And you live in Highgate as well do you?'

'No, I live in Archway, is just down the road. Is just one room, smaller than this place, but a lot cleaner.'

'So I take it you don't want a drink.'

'No we done with the coffee, is time for the movie.'

'I'll get the popcorn.'

'It's not that kind of entertainment.'

Barbara took a disk out of her handbag, handed it to Colin, who inserted it into the DVD player, Barbara saying:

'At least you have good TV.'

'At least that eh?'

The two of them sat on the sofa, Barbara lighting up. She gestured to the blankets folded at the end of the sofa:

'You don't even sleep with your wife no more?'

'She's not my wife any more. You ready?'

Barbara nodded, getting herself comfortable.

'You the one needs to be ready. What you about to see, it's something.'

Colin pressed 'play'.

Barbara was right. There was no credit sequence to prepare Colin. It was straight in, a low quality picture from a static camera up high. The judge naked on his back, arms outstretched, hands tied to the metal bedhead. Wearing nothing but the Judge's wig, Linda sitting on his face before lowering herself onto his cock.

Pangs of envy hit Colin. He thought they'd had great sex, at least when they'd first got together, but they'd never done any sort of bondage. Colin wanted to look away but was also strangely captivated.

Riding the judge hard, Linda's mouth was curled in mock anger. Colin just about made out her saying: "Fuck the judge, fuck the judge, fuck the judge." Over and over. Below her, the wigless judge was in ecstasy, groaning "yes, yes, yes."

Colin twisted in his seat uneasily, aroused despite himself. The judge had stamina, give him that.

'This go on for long?'

'Not long, ten more minutes.'

'Anything else happen?'

'No, just this.'

Colin pressed 'stop'. Barbara said:

'See enough hey?'

'You expect me to be shocked? I guessed as much.'

Colin wasn't sure how he felt. He wasn't that annoyed

or upset. He'd seen other men being seduced by Linda on film, but it was a different seeing her actually fucking another man. What he really felt was an aching sorrow for both of them. Any dreams they'd had, their marriage, adventure – all well and truly down the drain.

In one way it didn't matter to Colin any more, Linda no longer meant anything to him. And he was pretty sure she wasn't in love with the judge, that he was being used and would get his down the line when Linda had got whatever it was she needed from him.

Colin pulled himself together, pushing the images of Linda's infidelity away for now:

'Ok, so now there's proof they're together, how does that help either of us?'

'Is what I was hoping you could help me with a plan how to use the movie. Can't be right the judge with woman whose case he is dealing with.'

'No, but first there was no problem with the case. It was straightforward. The judge didn't even have to help her. Second, if he gets in trouble for having sex with Linda and the case is brought back to court, I'll be brought back as well.'

'Must be some way we can use it.'

'Okay, I'll give it some thought. What about you, anything you can put on him?'

'I could say I tell the papers he promise to help me with visa, put him in compromising position, but like you, gets me in trouble too.'

'I still don't know why you need my help anyway?'

'I need help for new visa. Mine expired, I am illegal.'

'What makes you think I can do anything about that?'

'I don't know, maybe you know someone who help.'

'I didn't even know Brazilians had a problem with visas.'

'Is like this. When I arrive here, I have student visa, sign up for English course in dodgy school in Oxford Street…'

'What was it called?'

'Oxford School of English, Mr. Stephen Lewis this big fat sleazeball manager, always try to have a feel of his students, you know it?'

Colin shrugged:

'Yea, you might say that, he was one of the people we did over.'

'Well only good thing about school is easy to help you for visa. I register, pay for course but never go. Nobody knows. I here to work, get some money. I do three years of study back in Rio. I don't want to study more.

'But student visa only let you work twenty hours a week. I get few jobs cleaning, do more than that, but have to be cash in hand. Then I become lover of the judge, so money no problem, but, I need work visa. The judge he say he sort this for me, he speak with people in immigration. But nothing happen.'

Colin nodded, lost in thought as Barbara went on:

'Your wife come, the judge he forget all about me. Now

I have no visa. Here as illegal. So I need visa and I need revenge for broken promise and I need money to make up for what I don't get any more.'

Barbara finished her monologue, inhaled on her cigarette, blew out smoke. Colin didn't say anything. He was taking time to digest everything Barbara had said and once he had, still wasn't sure how to formulate a plan. He asked:

'Where's the camera?'

'In the ceiling.'

'Do you think she knows it's there?'

'How I know?'

'When you and the judge did it, did you know?'

'No, he thinks is his secret, but I am his cleaner, I know his whole house, I find it all on the computer.'

Colin pressed 'play' again, the film continuing from where they left it, Linda still on top. Colin couldn't believe Linda would fall for it twice, but she didn't look as if she was playing to the camera.

Seeing Linda in the judge's wig reminded Colin of the time in her flat in Tokyo when she'd put on the Madonna wig. It made her face look different. It was some American actress she looked like. She wasn't 'A' list that was for sure. 'B', maybe even 'C'. Still couldn't think of the name though. Barbara interrupted Colin's thoughts:

'Is pretty but no much mamas.'

Colin stopped himself from asking what she meant,

guessing it wasn't mamas as in papas.

'I don't think she knows she's being filmed.'

'How does that help us?'

'If he's doing it against her knowledge, we can set them against each other. And go with your idea of threatening to expose it to the courts unless they give you money.'

Colin thinking out loud:

'The judge will have the most to lose, but it will probably throw Linda's plan out, which can only be a good thing.'

'You said if we do that you also go back to court.'

'Yes but she won't know I'm involved and you won't actually take it to the papers, it's a bluff.'

The film came to an abrupt end, the screen going blank. Colin turned off the DVD player. Barbara stubbed out her cigarette.

'You want to show me the bedroom?'

'Eh?'

'You just watch your wife have sex with the judge. He used to be with me, she used to be with you. So you want to foder? Do it in the bed where she sleeps.'

Colin saw her logic, could see the revenge they would get, so led the way. Before he knew it, she had her top off, saying:

'So which you prefer, mine or hers?'

Barbara's were definitely a lot bigger, but Colin didn't make a move, Barbara frowning:

'You just going to look at them?'

'No, because you're going to put your top back on.'

'You see these and you don't want to do anything. You a gay boy really? Was a fake marriage with your wife?'

'Look, I've just got other things on my mind.'

He was trying to be cool about it, but the fact was he just couldn't bring himself to do it. Any other time in his life sure, what man wouldn't, but right then he couldn't.

'And I told you we aren't husband and wife anymore.'

'Still legally married aren't you?'

'Ok, on paper we are still married but that's the only thing which shows we are. So you can stop calling her my wife.'

'So what you want to call her?'

'I know what I'd like to call her.'

'She a big bitch hey?'

'You could say that.'

'You like to smack her one?'

"Smack Your Bitch Up", thought Colin, that was an old tune he hadn't heard for a while.

'How about "SYBU"?'

'What's that mean?'

'Short for Smack Your Bitch Up.'

Her top back on, Barbara shrugged:

'Well I still need that visa.'

'We'll sort it out, don't worry. I've thought of someone who can help.'

CHAPTER 10

Colin hadn't called Vinnie at all since he'd got back to London. But Vinnie was a mate, he'd understand. Colin phoned and Vinnie's voice came on, the North London accent that Colin remembered but more formal:

'Hello, Vincent Gardner speaking.'

'Vinnie?'

'Who's this?'

'It's Colin.'

'Colin, hey, got your card awhile back, where are you?'

'In London.'

'Cool, when did you arrive back?'

'Uh, about six months ago.'

'Six months. And this is the first time you call me?'

'I know mate, it's bad, it's a long story. I'll explain it to you later. You around?'

'Could be, though I'll have to change my plans. I mean it will be cool to see you, don't get me wrong, but seeing as you waited six months, what's the sudden hurry?'

'Uh, I need a favour.'

'So let me see how this is. You've been here six months and you don't call your old mate Vinnie, then suddenly you need a favour, you remember him, that right?'

'Look, I've been meaning to call, it's just...I can't explain it over the phone.'

'Hey come on, just kidding you, what are mates for? Come on over. You know where I am?'

'The same address I sent the postcard to? Holloway Road?'

'That's it. Where you coming from, so I know how long you're going to be.'

'Tooting.'

'Bottom of the Northern Line?'

'Yea, almost.'

'See you in two days' time then.'

It didn't take Colin and Barbara two days to get from Tooting Broadway to Leicester Square, but long enough, twelve stops on the Northern Line, then change onto the Piccadilly and another six stops, before finally coming out of Holloway tube station.

Almost directly ahead was the way through to the new Arsenal Stadium. To the right were El Prado - Spanish Deli and the University of North London. To the left were the Nags Head and Morrisons. Middle class Islington one way, low class Holloway to the other.

Vinnie's place was just across the road, Blue Sky - Media Design. Colin and Barbara entered through the glass door, into a small reception area, a counter running across. Behind, a back room could be seen with computers and printers in.

A bald head turned, black and shiny, a rough smile breaking out in Vinnie's rugged face as he clicked off what he was doing. Vinnie was a stocky guy, smart white shirt strained by his weight-trained arms as he made his way into the reception, lifted up a flap in the counter, grabbed Colin's hand, and slapped him on the shoulder:

'Hey, good to see you man.'

'You too.'

'Why it took you so long to call hey?'

'Look, I…'

'Okay, okay, just kidding. I wish I could say you looked great, but you look a bit pale.'

'Hey, you too.'

Vinnie gave Colin a mock look of disapproval, then went back to his smile as he turned his attention to Barbara:

'And this must be the lucky lady you got hitched to?'

Colin and Barbara answered simultaneously:

'No she's…'

'No I'm…'

Colin tried again:

'This is…'

Barbara overrode him:

'I'm Barbara.'

Vinnie took her in, then turned back to Colin:

'Uh, okay…you want to get a drink?'

They went to a cafe next door, Vinnie saying "hi" to the girl who worked there, then turning back to Colin and Barbara:

'What do you want?'

'I'll get them.'

'Na, come on, Barbara?'

'Latte please.'

'Colin?'

'I'll have an espresso.'

Vinnie ordered the drinks, a juice for himself, then paid for them. The three of then sat by the window, Colin gesturing outside to the array of nationalities that passed by:

'Right mix around here isn't it?'

'Yea, you've got Albanians trying to sell you duty free packs of cigarettes on one side, Spanish delis offering you imported 'jamon' on the other. I'm like a bridge bringing the two sides together.'

'That's very noble of you – I always had you down as a socialist.'

'Yea, well the real reason is it's cheap to rent around here but it's also up and coming, Islington trying to spread its wings. Plus, the new Emirates Stadium around the corner. And I know the area. I grew up in Arsenal, just off Blackstock Road.'

He really did know it like the back of his hand. It had changed slightly while he'd been on the cruise ships, but once he was back, he just slipped into North London life. Seven Sisters Road was still the same poverty-littered dive it had always been and Upper Street was still inhabited by posh wankers.

Brought up by a single mum, bless her socks wherever she now resided - the ground probably as Vinnie didn't believe in heaven or hell. Far as he was concerned, life was just here on earth so you did with it what you could. Vinnie had shopped in Morrisons as a kid. Now he went to Waitrose, partly for the better quality food, partly for the posh totty to be picked up.

Holloway Odeon still stood out proudly on the corner, a grand building amid the run-down line of newsagents and internet cafes. Vinnie had lost his virginity in that cinema during a screening of Pulp Fiction. Had to go back and watch it the next day as he'd missed the action while getting some action.

His working class upbringing had made Vinnie tough and street-savvy, but he was smart enough to know where the money was. The University of North London had expanded, staff and student design needs kept him busy. And he'd been quick to offer his services to the new Arsenal consortium. Football was a whole new game these days. He was small scale in Arsenal's global marketing, but someone had to create their website. And he was that man, gaining a lucrative contract.

As for the Albanians, Vinnie knew more about them than his passing comment let on. It wasn't just their cigarettes that were illegal, some of the guys themselves were not officially in the country, knowledge that was profitable.

Colin gestured to Vinnie's attire:

'So what's with this new look white shirt and all.'

'I'm a business man now.'

'And you shaved off the dreads.'

'Yea, that's what you got to do man once you start losing it, looks like you're getting thinner on top yourself.'

'I know and only just thirty. I think it was in Japan, kept hitting my head on all the low doorframes.'

Colin and Vinnie were getting into the swing of old mate banter, Barbara with no option but to be quiet, quieter than she'd been the whole day with Colin. She had taken out a cigarette but remembered she could no longer smoke in public places, so was tapping it nervously against her leg. She couldn't keep quiet any longer, casting an admiring glance at Vinnie's arms:

'You go to the gym?'

'Just twice a week.'

Colin said:

'Don't remember you used to.'

'Can't stay the same all the time can you. How long's it been since we last saw each other?'

'Two years I guess.'

Vinnie turned to Barbara:

'We used to be on the cruise ships together.'

'Before I went to Tokyo and you came back here.'

'Good times.'

Vinnie turning again to Barbara:

'The two of us were in charge of all the media on deck.'

'I took the photos.'

'And I processed them and printed out leaflets for events on board. Remember how we had to do everything in one little room. Had that one machine – it was an all in one printer, scanner, copier – did everything on it…

'Stuff we used to get up to. Remember that time the two Swiss women had us taking photos of them in the nude, then relented. Didn't want their husbands seeing what was on the film, so we had to edit what was on there, for a price.'

'Yea, and when they said it was too steep, we gave them an alternative.'

'And what about the time when you fell for that old trick with the Austrian woman, falsely accused of taking her money the next day, reported to the manager, you were going to be kicked off. I had to say you'd been with me the whole time.'

Vinnie turned once again to Barbara:

'Always got in trouble with women. Don't know how he would have survived without me.'

Colin was starting to remember why he had taken so long to call Vinnie. Sure he was a great mate, but it had always been the same, Vinnie acting like an older brother, making him feel small.

They finished their drinks and went back into Vinnie's place, Vinnie lifting up the counter flap:

'Step into my office.'

The three of them moved into the back room, Vinnie gesturing to the various PCs and printing machines:

'As you can see it's a bit different from the old cruise ships.'

'Quite a set-up, doing good business?'

'I'm making forty thousand a year, not fantastic but it takes a few years for the business to grow. I'm my own boss and this is the second year. I've got an assistant I get to come in when I've got a heavy workload.'

'What do you design?'

'Websites, leaflets, posters. I've just got a new contract to revamp the Arsenal website.'

Vinnie wheeled two chairs over for Colin and Barbara, and sat in one himself,

'So let's get down to business. What's this favour you need?'

'Barbara needs a visa.'

Barbara explained:

'Mine run out. Was a student visa but I need a work visa.'

'How come you didn't get an extension?'

'I was promised new visa but person who promised is lying bastard.'

'You know what you're asking me to do is illegal?'

'I will pay for it.'

'I'm sorry, but I don't do that kind of stuff. I've got a nice business set up here, don't want to ruin it. I can't help you.'

Vinnie turned to Colin:

'No hard feelings eh. Look, I've got to finish off a few things. Come back at six and we'll have a drink.'

Colin stood up to leave. Vinnie stood up as well. They shook hands. Vinnie patted Colin on the shoulder, then gestured for Colin to raise his arms. Colin didn't know what was going on but raised his arms. Vinnie patted Colin down, feeling around his hoody top, hip pockets, jeans legs.

Vinnie turned to Barbara, about to gesture for her to stand with arms and legs apart, but she was already ready. Vinnie smiled as he searched her as well, Barbara enjoying being patted down, Vinnie enjoying doing it.

Satisfied, Vinnie sat back down:

'Just checking. Maybe one of you was wired up, trying to catch me out, record me doing something illegal, put it on one of those undercover documentaries, Panorama or some shit. I know you're an old friend, but you never know.'

Barbara was sitting back down, cigarette in hand, smiling. Vinnie said:

'Afraid you can't smoke in here either, being business premises. Upstairs in my flat is no problem.'

'No worry, I am just holding it for later.'

'So you need a work visa stamped in your passport?'

'Yes, another year so I can work, make some money, then I go back to Brazil.'

Colin was still standing, adjusting to what had just happened. Vinnie turned to him:

'Okay, so how does this involve you?'

'It's a long story…'

Barbara was back to her chatterbox self, interrupting Colin:

'His wife she run off to fodendo the judge.'

'She's hardly my wife anymore.'

'You still married aren't you?'

'Yes but…'

'So is still your wife. He don't like to admit that his wife leave him.'

'Hey I'm not the only one who was left. You didn't mention that you and the judge were together.'

'Okay so we were together, big deal, now is over, all I want is my visa and my money he owes me.'

Vinnie tried to calm proceedings:

'Okay, okay, straighten things out for me. What judge and how did you two get together?'

Barbara got in before Colin:

'I was cleaner for the judge. Also his lover. He promise to get my visa but don't do it because he too busy fucking his wife. The judge was doing their case, so I see them both in court, suggest we can help each other.'

Vinnie's head turned once more to Colin:

'I feel like I'm watching tennis here. What were you doing in court?'

'We got taken to court for attempted blackmail and extortion.'

'But you won or you wouldn't be here.'

'The case was dismissed due to new evidence. But SYBU was trying to frame me for it.'

'Who the hell is SYBU?'

'That's what I call her.'

'Who?'

Barbara rolled her eyes, butting in:

'His wife...'

'That's her actual name?'

'No. Linda Croswell, maiden name Collins.'

Vinnie nodding as he turned back to Colin:

'Or Colin's Linda. Why do you call her SYBU?'

'Short for Smack Your Bitch Up.'

Vinnie rubbed the back of his head:

'Okay, I think I get the general idea. So now Barbara's helping you get revenge on your wife – Linda - SYBU - while you help her get revenge on the judge.'

Vinnie turned once more to Barbara:

'You got this passport on you so I can get a visa printed in?'

Barbara got it out of her handbag, handed it over. Vinnie placed the passport on his desk, said:

'Give me until tomorrow morning.'

Colin said:

'I've got a few things I need to check tomorrow, so might be a bit later.'

'Ok, come up when you're done, we'll have lunch.'

Barbara asked:

'Is okay if I come earlier to pick it up, I live just up the road?'

'Sure, why not.'

Barbara smiled coyly, turned and sashayed out of the premises, the men watching her. Colin and Vinnie shook hands a third time, Vinnie with his broad crooked smile:

'Man, she'll take your mind off a cheating ex-wife alright.'

Colin said nothing, not wanting Vinnie to know he'd let the opportunity of sex with Barbara slip by. And knowing Vinnie as the predator he was, Colin would no doubt be hearing of his conquest within the next few days. Same as he'd had to listen to all Vinnie's sexual stories the whole time on the ships.

Outside, Barbara had lit up and was joyfully exhaling smoke. Colin said:

'Okay, so you're going to get your visa.'

'Yes, your friend is very generous.'

She didn't think to thank Colin for organising it. He said:

'I'm going to check out the judge myself tomorrow, then the day after we can put it to them.'

'Whenever you ready.'

Barbara shrugged, dropped her sunglasses down into place and walked up Holloway Road. Vinnie could be good, she thought, she liked how he worked.

Colin made his way to the tube station, only to find the gates had shut. The station temporarily closed due to lift failure. Bloody underground. Making his way to Highbury, Colin was lost in thought as he walked. Only the day before, he had been on his own, nobody else involved. But as Linda had first got Hugh on her side, then the judge, he might as well get Barbara and Vinnie in with him. At least no harm in them knowing. Was there?

CHAPTER 11

First thing in the morning, Colin was in Café Nero on Vernon Place, waiting for Hugh to come out of Holborn Station on his way to the office. Hugh appeared, crossing the street, a wide plaster on the bridge of his nose, his left eye blackening. Colin stood up. Hugh rolled his eyes dramatically:

'If you're thinking of getting rough again, forget it. I've forgiven you for yesterday, you were angry. Do it again and I'll have the police on you in minutes.'

'I'm sorry about yesterday – guess I need an anger management course. I just need some information.'

'It's over Colin. You won the case. Forget it. I suspect it is also over between you and Linda. My advice would be to forget that too. Best you can both do is amicably agree to split the money. And that advice is free.'

'I haven't come about the case or Linda. I want to know about our judge – Judge Stephenson.'

'What about him?'

'Where can I find him? Is he down in Southwark? On any particular case?'

'Look, I don't know what it is you hope to gain...'

'I just want to see him in action. I thought he was good.'

Hugh sighed. Colin was obviously up to something, but it didn't really matter. All Hugh wanted was to be rid of him. He had an important client due in first thing.

And besides, the case Judge Stephenson was on was hardly a secret, so he might as well tell Colin:

'Yes, Judge Stephenson is down in Southwark. He's doing the Stockwell Three case. It's all over the newspapers.'

'Ok, thanks, and I'm sorry again about your nose.'

Hugh watched Colin walk off to the tube station. Now that he remembered, a few weeks prior to the court date Linda had also been asking him about the judge, but in a more subtle way. Who knew what they were both up to? Shaking his head in dismay at the people he came into daily contact with, Hugh went into his office building.

On the tube, Colin picked up a crumpled Metro. Sure enough, on the front page was the headline "Stockwell Three Sentence Today". Colin read the article. Three black youths from Stockwell had raped a black girl also from Stockwell. But not only that, they had caught the whole thing on their mobile phone video cameras, sending it to their friends and even putting it on Facebook and YouTube. The three of them weren't hard to trace.

It was obviously big news and had been so for some time, the main article followed by another about black on black crime in the Capital, but this was the first Colin had heard of it. It just went to show how he had been living in his own little world. When Colin and Linda had been busy planning and executing their blackmail plots, that was all he'd thought about. And once it had all gone wrong, his mind had been occupied with working out what it was Linda was scheming. Even now, they were apart, she was consuming all his waking thoughts.

The court was packed, unlike the day before when Colin and Linda had been in. Apparently there had been a day recess, which is how Judge Stephenson must have been able to preside over Colin and Linda's case.

Colin managed to squeeze into the spectators gallery, the place was full of TV crews', journalists, photographers, the families of the accused and victim, cameras flashing and voices rising. In the dock were the three boys, all seventeen, each flanked by security guards.

Colin overheard a conversation between some of the journalists:

'Can't believe he's let us lot all in, we never normally get into a case like this.'

'There'll be some reason behind it, you know Judge Stephenson.'

Judge Stephenson entered from the back with a swish of his gown. The clerk banged his hammer:

'Order in the court, order in the court.'

Everyone fell silent. Judge Stephenson looked directly at the boys:

'As you are aware, a verdict of guilty was reached the day before yesterday. Today is simply to confirm the sentence.

'What you did was unspeakable. You have caused irreparable damage to this young girl and her family. She has shown remarkable bravery in appearing in person.

You will see that I have taken the unusual step of allowing the media into court.

'I have done this to set an example. You are all three over the age limit. You will receive the maximum penalty of ten years imprisonment.

'Unfortunately I am unable to impose life, otherwise I would. But your faces will be caught on camera; will appear in Newspapers and on TV screens nationwide. You are being named and shamed as the rapists that you are. Nobody will ever forget the vile act that you have committed. Court dismissed.'

And with that Judge Stephenson exited with a flourish. Immediately cries of joy and sadness arose from the opposing families, cameras flashed once more, security hurriedly ushered the three defendants out of the court.

In the hubbub of people leaving the gallery, Colin listened to journalists swapping information:

'You know that the youngest only just turned seventeen yesterday, that's why the judge deliberately delayed the sentence by a day.'

'He couldn't have created a more dramatic outcome.'

'But is it really to prove a point or is it just that he likes his own face in the paper?'

'Good point.'

Colin left the press milling around the outside of the court, wondering what he had learnt. Not much apart from that his and Linda's case was nothing in the big scale of things. And as for the judge, he liked to be in the limelight, but Colin wasn't sure how that helped him know what Linda was up to. God, he hated this. Why did they have to hate each other? Okay, it was over. Couldn't she just agree to fifty per cent and they could both get on with their lives? But he knew there was no chance of that.

It was nearly lunch time by the time Colin reached Holloway Road. He entered Blue Sky - Media Design, Vinnie turning to see who it was, and calling over:

'Hey Colin, come on through, won't be a second.'

Colin lifted the counter flap and went into the back room where Vinnie was at work on some website. Colin sat down and waited while Vinnie finished off what he was doing. Over his shoulder, Vinnie said:

'So what you been up to?'

'I was down in Southwark Court, big case there, Stockwell Three, heard of them?'

'Course I've heard of them, it's been in the newspapers every day for the last month.'

Vinnie clicked off what he was doing and spun around in his chair:

'Well you want to know what I've been doing? I spent my morning trying to make a deal with Barbara about payment for her visa.'

'She's been already has she?'

'She was here first thing. I'd just finished the visa. Looks cool by the way, just like the real deal. Nobody will know the difference. Just if somebody actually checks on the system, sees she shouldn't have a visa and then asks her how she's got one.

'Anyway, I'm showing her the visa printed on her passport, when she asks if there is any way that she could persuade me to lower the price, which I haven't even told her yet.

'So I said I could probably be persuaded. And down she goes to lick the old lollipop. Then a couple of minutes in, she stops, starts to haggle, asking for fifty percent reduction. I told her to get back down there. She starts again, then comes back, says "never mind, I want what you've got."

'Takes her top off – man have you seen the size of them? And puts her arse in the air. I told her if I'm giving her pleasure, she aint getting any discount. She said she don't care. So I end up giving it to her from behind for no discount.'

Vinnie didn't tell Colin that afterwards he'd told Barbara she didn't have to pay, just to remember that she owed him a favour. Vinnie smiling:

'Can you believe this lady? Sure know where I'm going on holiday next year. Brazilian women man…remember that Maria on the ship?'

Colin wasn't going to answer the last question, Vinnie seemingly oblivious to the hurt it had caused Colin two years previous. And he wasn't too thrilled to be hearing about something he'd stupidly declined, but he tried not to show it:

'So not a bad deal then?'

Vinnie getting into his stride, like the old days back on the ships:

'See, white girls are better for blow jobs coz they got smaller lips, black girls got better arses.'

'So what you want is a mixture, half and half right?'

'As long as it's the right way around. You don't want a black girl's lips with a white girl's arse.'

'But Barbara is kind of mulatto though.'

'Yea, but not enough. But you must have had a go with her as well no?'

'She offered, but I…'

'Man, what's with you, she's right, you're still not over this wife, sorry SYBU. You hungry? Come on, let's get some lunch.'

As they walked up Holloway Road, Vinnie said:

'Food's better at the deli but if we're going to talk, better to go to Nag's Head. We can be anonymous there, nobody notices that you're in, or too drunk to notice anyway.'

Opposite the Nag's Head was the Odeon, advertising the third film in the Pirates of the Caribbean series. Colin hadn't even seen the first one. More and more he was starting to think he was behind the times.

Inside the dark, stale alcohol smelling pub, Vinnie insisted on buying again:

'You want a drink?'

'Sure, why not, a pint of whatever you're getting.'

Vinnie arrived at the table with a pint of lager for Colin and a juice for himself. Colin looked at Vinnie disbelievingly:

'You not drinking?'

'Na, don't drink anymore.'

'You've really changed.'

'People do Colin, you've got to move on mate. Those days on the cruise ships were good times, but the days of snorting coke and getting drunk are behind me. See that's your problem, you're still the same, you don't adapt.

'I mean look at you, you were wearing the same kind of hoody top back then. You probably still listen to the same old shit, what was it, Stone Roses, and it was out of date even then.'

Colin shifted uncomfortably as Vinnie put a final dig in:

'And without me, you're still getting into trouble with women.'

Vinnie paused as the food was served by a bored-looking bar girl, beef burger for Colin, veggie burger for Vinnie. When the girl left, Vinnie said:

'So, are you going to tell me the whole story?'

Colin told Vinnie the whole story. Getting married in Vegas, it not working out in Mexico, depressed back in London, starting the blackmail scams, the excitement and passion back, but then starting to argue, until one of the scams went wrong. It all starting to unravel so fast and then the final most recent installment of the judge and Barbara entering the scene.

Vinnie asked the important question:

'So how much have you got in the bank?'

'About two hundred thousand, give or take.'

'Why don't you just split it?'

'If only it was that easy - it's all or nothing with her. Either she gets it or I do. Money's in a joint account. Neither of us can take any out unless we've got both signatures. I mean we can take up to fifty quid a day from cash machines, but it will take awhile that way to get the money.'

'Where's she from?'

'Manchester.'

'I could have told you not to trust a northern girl. They're good for a good time, but you don't marry them. Like that girl, what was her name?'

Colin knew exactly who Vinnie was referring to. Jo, a strapping Yorkshire lass who was on a honeymoon cruise, but unable to resist Vinnie's charms. Not needing to be reminded of any more of Vinnie's conquests, Colin wasn't going to help out with her name. Better to keep the focus on himself:

'Well it's too late now.'

'And how the hell did you go along with her plan in the first place.'

'Come on, you and me used to get up to similar things

on the cruises.'

'Like I said, things change. Look at the Arsenal. I used to go and watch them when I was a kid at Highbury. Now, Even if I had the time, I can hardly afford tickets. Players, they get the money you're talking about in one week. But it's no use complaining. That's how things have changed, so you've got to find your own opportunities.'

'Why should I do a job I don't like if I can work out another way to make money? I tell you, I don't feel guilty about any of those bastards we took money from.'

'You're talking like a kid, like those Stockwell Three, imagining they're some gangsta rappers, above the law.'

'So you're mister innocent business man these days are you, never take an opportunity if it came up?'

'I'm not saying I'd turn it down, but you've got to have something else in place, something to fall back on, just in case. You could have a got a job with me for example, at least as a cover.'

Colin was silent, reprimanded, playing with the beer mat. Vinnie rubbed the back of his shaved head, relented:

'Ok, so how are you planning to get the money?'

'I don't know. She's up to something with the judge. Barbara's going to blackmail the two of them with the video of them together. That way, she'll get the money she wants and SYBU will have to come to me for help. I'll say I'll help as long as she signs for me to take the money out.'

'And why were you watching the judge in action

today?'

'See if I could find out anything useful, but apart from the fact that he likes publicity, I didn't learn much.'

There was a lot to be learnt, thought Vinnie. The judge liked publicity, but where there was good publicity there could also be bad publicity. Somebody would soon realise that. As for Colin's plan, it sounded a bit vague to Vinnie, but he didn't say that. Sometimes it was best just to keep quiet and see how things turned out.

CHAPTER 12

Colin and Barbara were sat by the window in the coffee shop in Highgate, Barbara with a latte in front of her, Colin an espresso. It was most definitely a coffee shop not a café, the place all cappuccino and carrot cake, at Highgate prices. But the location was perfect, being halfway down Southwood Lane, on the corner of Kingsley Place.

They didn't have much to say to each other, but it didn't bother either of them. Barbara had had her fill with Vinnie, thinking she would go along with Colin's plan, but if she needed to ditch it at any point, she would. Colin was watching the road, playing with the tea spoon by the side of his cup.

Judge Stephenson's yellow VW came into view, stopping at the turning, right outside the coffee shop. Oblivious to the fact that he was being watched, the judge turned his curly head left then right, checking the road was clear before pulling out and disappearing out of sight.

Colin turned to Barbara:

'Okay, he's gone.'

Barbara lazily had another slurp of her latte before standing. Colin couldn't but help notice her breasts pushing out her top, this time covered in bright yellow and blue zig zags. Maybe he'd been stupid to turn down the opportunity.

'So let's go over the plan one more time...'

Barbara rolled her eyes as she stopped him from finishing:

'Is simple. I go in, show your wife the video, ask for money.'

'But you don't mention me.'

'No, I don't mention you. Is just between me and them. Then she come to you for help with the money.'

'I'll be waiting here.'

Barbara shrugged as she left the coffee shop, cigarette in hand, handbag over shoulder, sunglasses on head.

Outside, Barbara lit up the cigarette that had been waiting in her hand, inhaled and slid her sunglasses down for the short one minute walk down Kingsley Place.

Outside number six, Barbara stood having a last few drags. She looked up at the French windows that opened onto a balcony with a sweeping view of the city. Standing behind the glass was Linda, coffee in hand, taking in the view.

The two women saw each other, eyes offering a slight acknowledgement. Barbara tossed away her cigarette butt and tottered over to the front door. Linda guessed that Barbara was the cleaner, due in that morning so didn't go down to open the door.

Barbara had a key, but rang the doorbell. It took a while before Linda opened the door, a forced smile as she said:

'Hi he said you'd be here to do the cleaning, but I

thought you had your own key.'

'I do.'

'Oh, well I'll leave you to it.'

Linda started to turn, leaving Barbara to come in and shut the door behind her, but was brought to a halt as Barbara said:

'I don't come here to clean, I came here to see you.'

Barbara sashayed into the house, leaving Linda to close the door. Facing the door, Linda's lips curled in thought. She turned to face Barbara with a fake smile:

'Well have a seat. Coffee? Tea? Not that I'd recommend the tea, he drinks Early Grey. But then you must know that.'

'Coffee please.'

Barbara made herself comfortable in the lounge, a white leather designer sofa on Moroccan tiled flooring. In the kitchen Linda made coffee, pressing down the plunger in the cafetiere. Not expecting anyone apart from the cleaner, Linda was in plain jeans, no make-up on. Barbara was fully dolled up, obviously trying to get the upper hand. Trying to reverse the roles of cleaner and guest.

Linda brought the coffee in on a tray:

'Help yourself to milk and sugar. I'll be back in a minute.'

Linda heading upstairs, where she briefly applied mascara and lipstick, pouted her mouth as she looked in the mirror. That would do. She picked up the fake passport the judge had dubiously acquired for her. Sure he was a middle aged pervert, but he'd come through. Getting a bit clingy and now that she had what she needed, no point hanging around. Just had to get her bloody money from Colin and she was off somewhere hot. Somewhere where Colin would never be able to find her, so she could escape an abusive husband – that's how she'd played it to the judge.

Downstairs, Barbara was deciding how to play the opening move. Initially she took out the disc with the home movie on, thinking to leave it on the coffee table for when Linda came back down, but then decided that wouldn't have enough impact, so put it back in her handbag.

Linda casually came back down into the lounge, and sat opposite Barbara:

'So, what is it that you wanted to see me about?'

'I have something might interest you.'

'Really?'

Barbara took out the disc from her handbag, looked at it then across at Linda:

'You want to know what is on here?'

'I'm sure you're going to tell me.'

'Is home movie of you and the judge, doing a bit of a sexy act.'

'I don't think so.'

'You don't think so? We can watch if you want. Or maybe I give you picture - you on top, wearing his wig...'

Linda's mouth turned down:

'So maybe you have some home movie. And the point is?'

'Point is maybe you and the judge don't want for anyone to see. Just few days ago you had court case with him as the judge. Would look very bad anyone knows. But nobody has to.'

'If, let me guess, money is paid.'

'Let's say twenty thousand.'

Linda's mouth started to sneer:

'Did Colin put you up to this?'

There was a seconds hesitation before Barbara replied:

'No, is my own idea.'

How had Linda guessed so quickly, wondered Barbara. Colin, so clever, hadn't said what to do if Linda brought his name up, just said not to mention him. And she realised, she'd said it was her own idea, but what she should have said was "who's Colin?"

Linda had latched on:

'So you did talk with him?'

It was too late to deny it so Barbara said:

'I talked with him yes, but is nothing to do with him.'

'Look, I don't know what Colin has told you, but blackmail won't work. First, the court case has already been concluded. Even if it was brought back to court, so would he. You can try it on the judge but it won't work on me.'

Linda settled back in the white leather armchair.

Barbara was no longer in control. The bluff had failed instantly. She had to think quickly how to repair the situation, but Linda was already asking a question:

'I would like to know though how you got a film of us.'

'I just come across it.'

Linda took a guess:

'Were you and the judge together?'

'I'm not after him back, he's velha cabra, I just want what he owes me.'

Linda got the gist:

'I didn't think you could be in love with an old fool like him.'

'So what you doing with him then?'

'Probably same as you were. You had a good thing going eh? Money, clothes?'

'Well it was pretty good.'

'Hey, I'm with you. A girl has to use her assets. Look, I'm going to be honest with you. I doubt Colin told you the truth about us. We got in serious trouble. I didn't want any part of his blackmail schemes, but he forced me to do it, physically threatened me. Even made me go with other men so that we could claim sexual harassment. What kind of husband does that?'

Linda almost starting to believe the story herself. Barbara squinted at her:

'Is true? He tell me something different. Say you make him cornear, wear the horns, go with the judge to get his money.'

'I don't know what Colin's told you Barbara, but when the court case came up, yes I tried to protect myself, so I got in with the judge. I'm still here just to see what more I can get out of it. But I'm done here, there's nothing else for me. He didn't tell me about you two. If I'd known, I would have got out of your way straight away. That's men for you.'

Barbara nodded. In her experience all men were bastards. Either sticking a gun or their dick in your face. Sometimes both at the same time.

'You know what I think, I think we should put our female minds together. See if we can't both get something out of this situation.'

Barbara took it in. She didn't have any affiliation with Colin. Linda had seen through his plan straight away, and was obviously smarter. And she wasn't the bitch he'd made her out to be. But Barbara couldn't simply give in, so she arched her back proudly, breasts out. Linda had already noticed them. Barbara wasn't as pretty as she was, but she had a pretty good figure and amazing breasts.

Linda took the initiative:

'You want money to make up for what you've lost by me coming onto the scene right? Well I've got an idea. Are there also films of you and him?'

'Yes, is all on his computer.'

'You knew he was filming you?'

'I found out. He thinks I'm stupid Brazilian cleaner,

just good for fodenda. I study computers in Rio. I know more than he does. I know his house more than he does. He at work, I go on and see what I can find.'

'Can you show me?'

'Sure.'

Linda let Barbara lead the way upstairs, in the house she knew so well. At the doorway to the bedroom, Barbara leaned in, pointed to the top corner:

'You see, is very small, I didn't know was there either until I found movie on computer.'

Linda saw the tiny camera in the ceiling. She couldn't believe that she'd been caught out twice. Well, she'd finished with the judge, he'd get his comeuppance. And she wasn't going to show that she was upset by it.

On the computer in the judge's study, Barbara quickly found her way to the files she was looking for - 'Home Movies', listed were both of Barbara's and Linda's names, then a series of other ones – Gloria, Alessandra, Tom, surely a typo there, Mona…

Linda asked:

'Well you've seen me, so can I see you?'

'Sure why not.'

Barbara moved the mouse to click on one of the files with her name attached, pressed 'play'. The screen showed an almost identical scene to the one of Linda, Barbara on top of the judge, wearing a wig.

Difference was Barbara's breasts. They really were something, holding up round and firm even out of her top. Linda was impressed:

'I've got to ask you, are they one hundred percent real?'

'You bet one hundred percent natural.'

'Uh, I couldn't see what they're like to feel could I?'

'Sure, Go ahead.'

Barbara turned her chest to Linda, who cupped them admiringly:

'Amazing. You know if I get enough money, I'm going to get myself some.'

Linda took her hands away. Barbara gestured to the monitor screen:

'Is enough?'

'Yea, he doesn't have much imagination does he? Getting both of us to do exactly the same thing.'

'Is what turns him on. Nearly all others same too, apart from this one.'

Barbara clicking on 'Tom'. At first, the young Asian body looked female, but turning around, Tom was clearly a Thai guy. As for the judge, he was not only tied to the bed, but had metal pegs on his nipples and a gag in his mouth. Just as Tom stood over the judge and started to urinate, Linda clicked the film off. If that got into the public domain it would certainly be embarrassing for the judge but it wasn't illegal:

'You know we should show him, like I said, put our female minds together. Using the film with me in isn't going to do anything. But you could use the film with you in.'

Barbara looked at Linda suspiciously:

'I do that, my name will be all over papers as well.'

'But you don't actually do it, just threaten to. It's the same as your original plan, but with the judge, not me. See, with me it's not much of a big deal. With you, he has a lot more to lose. You've got him by the balls, you just need to squeeze and watch the money fall out of his pockets.'

Barbara thought out loud:

'Suppose I could now that I don't need him for my visa. He owes me, big time.'

Linda took in Barbara's comment about no longer needing a visa but didn't show it:

'He isn't going to want the publicity of having his cleaner as his lover, especially with the visa issue. Can you copy this onto a disc?'

'Sure.'

Barbara copied the film onto a disc, took the disc out of the computer, put it in her handbag. She was hesitant then took the disc with Linda on back out of the bag, offered it to Linda:

'Here, you might as well keep this now.'

'Thanks. I'm going to delete all the files with me on – you want yours deleted?'

'Sure, thanks.'

'I'll be out of here before he gets back tonight, so you can come by whenever you want.'

'I go home now. Wait till he finish work.'

Linda showed Barbara out of the house, the two of them kissing on the cheeks, girlfriends now.

Colin was waiting impatiently in the coffee shop. It was taking longer than it should. He'd ordered another espresso, double this time. Problem with espressos was that they were too small, too quick to drink. But he didn't like how milky a latte was or how frothy a cappuccino was. Couldn't anywhere just serve coffee, strong with a bit of milk?

The three hits of caffeine were almost like being back on the old cocaine in cruise ship days. He felt wired. Barbara came into view, sunglasses down, cigarette in hand. He started to relax. But she didn't come into the coffee shop. Walked straight past, didn't even acknowledge him.

Colin dashed out of the coffee shop, ran up to Barbara:

'Hey, what's going on?'

'I no need you anymore.'

'What? What the hell happened?'

'I have a new plan, one that don't involve you. I don't need a man who makes his wife go with other men. What kind of man is that? A cafetina is what! Maybe because you can't get it up eh? Impotente. Flacido penis. Eunuco.'

'Hey, that's not true. What's she been saying?'

Colin's mobile bleeped with a new text message. Barbara hurried on her way, heading for Highgate tube station. Colin started to go after her, but then stopped, looked at the text he'd received. It was from Linda:

"Nice try. By way, sleeping at flat 2nite, don't disturb."

A photo jpeg was attached of Colin naked apart from a wig, taken so long ago in Tokyo, Colin looking ridiculously like Jack Lemmon. Colin got the picture – a man dressed as a woman who doesn't get the girl. A token of Colin and Linda's old love turned into a mocking taunt.

CHAPTER 13

Mobile phone gripped in his hand, Colin stood on the bridge looking down at the traffic coming up from Holloway, under the bridge, through to the north circular until it came to the start of the M1, the sign by the side of the road there simply stating THE NORTH. He thought about Linda and wanted to rip that sign down.

There was an old bunch of flowers tied to the railings, for someone who'd jumped Colin guessed. He was feeling pretty shit, but he wouldn't be doing that. He wasn't going to let SYBU drive him to despair. A part of him wanted to wallow in self pity. He had genuinely fallen in love with Linda and he was pretty sure she had too. Maybe if they'd never started the scams it wouldn't have all gone wrong.

Now, she not only hated him, but was outwitting him at every turn. Hadn't she humiliated him enough? His anger mounted, replacing the sad feeling inside his gut. It was just a matter of how he could pay her back.

He snapped out of it, looked at the time on his mobile. He'd been there for nearly an hour. He started down, leaving Highgate - garden design vans driving away from plush premises, walking through Archway – drunks with bandaged heads staggering out of the hospital, and down Holloway Road – Albanians stepping out to offer tax free packs of cigarettes.

Reaching Blue Sky – Media Design, Colin went to push

the door open and found it locked. It wasn't lunch time yet. He called Vinnie on his mobile, Vinnie answering:

'Hey Colin.'

'You in?'

'Yea, where are you?'

'I'm outside.'

'Be down now.'

Vinnie opened the door, in a light blue shirt, but not perfectly tucked in, slightly dishevelled and out of breath. Colin was so angry he barely noticed:

'That's it, I'm going to kill her I swear.'

'You want a cup of tea or something.'

'No I don't want a cup of fucking tea.'

'Coffee?'

'Jesus, no, I've had three espressos already.'

'Okay, okay. Just trying to get you calmed down man. See, you're always acting on impulse. You want to tell me what happened?'

They were in the back part of the shop, Colin unable to keep still as he let it all out, barely pausing for breath:

'What happened is she's humiliated me one step too far. The plan backfired. I don't know what she said exactly to Barbara, but she guessed it was to do with me, then sent a text "nice try." Just to rub my nose in it'

'Man I told you those Northern girls, real schemers.'

'Well it's too late now.'

'So what you going to do now?'

'She also said in the text she's staying in the flat

tonight. She's obviously finished with the judge. Who knows what she's got Barbara to do. But I swear if I see her, I'll strangle her.'

'And then what?'

'What do you mean?'

'I mean I agree with you, she deserves everything she gets. Only so much a man should take. She's trying to get all of the money; she fucked another man while she was still married to you. Now she's trying to rub it all in. But killing her? Come on Col, it's just not you. What you need is a plan to get the money and then haul arse, get yourself away to some remote country with a nice beach, put it all behind you…'

'Yea, guess you're right. Always fancied Thailand…'

'Why Thailand?'

'I don't know. It's far away. Once I'm there, I can disappear.'

'Okay, Thailand. You got to buy the ticket, have a bit of money for when you arrive. How are you going to do that if you can't get more than fifty pounds out of the machine?'

'So what are you saying, don't do anything, let SYBU get away with it all?'

'Hey, I'm with you. You're my mate. In fact if you don't give it to her, I'll think you're not man enough. But I'm saying look at the practicalities - you need money…'

'But I told you I can't get access to it unless we both sign for it.'

'Just get someone else to sign instead of her.'

'Yea right, that easy.'

'Where did you set up the account?'

'In Tooting.'

'So all you do is go to some other branch, a main one, say in Piccadilly. Phone first to arrange it, then go in with another woman who signs as SYBU. They won't know what you look like, so long as the signature matches…'

'Jesus, why did I never think of that?'

Vinnie shrugged. Colin started to take the idea seriously:

'But who?'

'How about Barbara?'

'She won't do it, SYBU's set her against me somehow.'

'Yea, she will, once I talk with her. I'll go and get her down.'

'She's here?'

'Yea, she came for a quick one. Man the woman's mad for it. I just finished up when you called. She's probably having a shower. We'll see what she's got to say about what went on.'

Vinnie shouted up:

'Hey Barbara, you finished up there?'

'Uh huh.'

'You want to come on down.'

Barbara came bouncing down, happy with herself. Her happy attitude soon faded when she saw Colin with Vinnie. She sneered:

'Is the man with the plan. Like to send his wife to go with other men.'

Barbara with hands on hips as she launched into one:

'Um cafetina, impotente, flacido…'

'Whatever she told you, Linda made it up, it's what she does.'

Vinnie interrupted:

'Okay, what we want to find out here is what exactly happened. You got to remember Barbara, Colin is a very good mate of mine, we go all the way back. So what did you and SYBU talk about?'

'She said his plan no good, because case can't be brought back to court, so no use to threaten her. Instead better to threaten judge and squeeze his testicoles.'

'With what?'

'Movie of him and me.'

'Who's got that?'

'Me.'

'No copies?'

'His wife was deleting them.'

'Okay, here's a new plan, see how you all like this. Barbara forget about the judge for now. Plenty of time to take him down later. You've got your visa. And there's an easier way to get the money you've lost out on. Colin needs to get some money from his account with SYBU. Only way to do that is to have her signature. So you pose as his wife.'

'I don't want to be wife pretend or not of this cafetina.'

'If you remember Barbara you owe me a favour. So this is the favour. And, Colin will give you a percentage of the money won't you?'

Colin looked at Vinnie sceptically. Vinnie repeated himself:

'Won't you?'

Colin reluctantly nodded. Barbara looked far from happy, but nodded too. Vinnie continued:

'So if you're both agreed, this is what you do. Colin you need to get yourself a suit or something smart.'

'What for?'

'You going to walk into a bank like that and ask them to hand over two hundred grand in cash? No, so you need to get yourself down to Upper Street and get some decent clothes. You'll need a briefcase as well, for the money. Barbara meanwhile you can get down to Camden market, buy a couple of rings, so that it looks like you're married. And Colin, before you go, I need your bank card.'

Colin took his card out of his wallet, handed it over dubiously:

'Why do you need this?'

'So we can print out an identical one. Barbara signs the back as SYBU so that when the bank manager checks her signature on whatever you both sign it's the same. This card won't actually work in the machines, it's just to show to the manager. You need to act like you're husband and wife and make up some story as to why you need all the money in cash.'

Colin phoned to arrange the meeting with the bank, then went off to buy a suit and briefcase. Barbara left to get the rings. Vinnie made the bank card. The three of them lost in their own thoughts as they got on with their respective jobs. Barbara was easy. She'd gone from Colin's plan to Linda's no problem. She could just as easily swap to Vinnie's. You had to be adaptable. And Vinnie was most definitely the coolest, so it seemed a good idea to go along with him.

Colin accepted the plan, but he wasn't sure about the whole thing, wasn't sure one bit. He was no longer in control, things were moving too fast. There were too many people involved. And yet, what choice did he have, now that it had got this far?

Vinnie saw the whole thing heading for catastrophe unless he took charge. Colin was so impulsive, he probably would actually kill his wife, or SYBU as he called her. And she sounded like she was pretty cunning. He would place a bet on the judge and Barbara being in the papers by the next day. And as for Barbara, if she got in one bit of trouble, she would put herself first at whatever cost. What Vinnie had to do was take control without actually getting involved.

CHAPTER 14

Linda and Judge Stephenson were in the glass-fronted wine bar in Southwark, having met for lunch, the judge eagerly holding up a glass of red:

'One glass of wine never hurt anyone's judgement don't you think?'

Linda smiled back as they clinked glasses, Linda taking a sip before gushing gratitude:

'I want to thank you again for the passport. It's such a relief to know that I can escape his clutches. All the things he made me do, just for money.'

Linda shuddered:

'Oh, just remembering it makes me feel sick.'

She broke into a smile:

'But thanks to you, I'll finally be free of him.'

'Least I could do. But I don't understand why you don't just let me get an injunction. Prevent him from coming into contact that sort of thing.'

'You've done more than enough. Let's not talk about it anymore. So what about you, any interesting cases this morning?'

'Just a quick couple of court orders, nothing special. I spent most of it dealing with press enquiries about the Stockwell Three as it has now become known.'

The judge puffing himself up as if there were cameras around:

'I had an interview with James Littlewood, you know,

of the Standard.'

'I had an interesting morning. Barbara, the cleaner came around.'

'Oh yes, is the place nice and clean now?'

'She didn't do any cleaning, she came to talk to me.'

'What on earth about?'

'You didn't tell me that you two were lovers.'

'Uh well you know how it is. Besides, it was over long before you and I met.'

'That wasn't quite how she saw it. Said you just dumped her once I came on the scene. She seems to think that you owe her money.'

'Ridiculous!'

'She also said she has a film of you two together.'

'Impossible!'

'And she's planning to blackmail you with it. Either you pay up or she sends it to the papers. You know, prominent judge having sex with cleaner scandal.'

'Preposterous!'

'Is there a film of you and her having sex?'

'Well now you come to mention it, there might very well be. But I don't see how she can know about it. It's on a file on the computer.'

'So maybe she's just bluffing, doesn't actually have the film. If you tell me where, I can go and delete them.'

'Oh no need for you to worry about it,' the judge desperately searching for the best way out of this unsavoury situation:

'No need for you to get involved at all. I can do it.'

'I already am involved. And I think it's best to do it as soon as possible. She still has a key to the house doesn't she? Why don't you want me to see, is there something to hide?'

Linda enjoying his discomfort. The judge sheepishly explained:

'You see, the thing is, well it's just that, there's a film of you as well. A bit of harmless fun. I was going to tell you, but I didn't know how you would feel about it.'

'You're a very naughty judge, you know that. I might well have to give you the jolly good spanking you deserve.'

Judge Stephenson looked suitably sheepish. And also a little excited by the thought of being spanked by Linda, who didn't seem that angry:

'Okay, I'll have to punish you for that later. First we have to deal with Barbara. What did you promise her, a visa?'

'I might have vaguely mentioned it, but I didn't actually get one for her.'

'That's not very gentlemanly.'

'It was too complicated. It was impossible for me to get her one without my name coming up somewhere.'

'You managed to get me one without much problem.'

'You are already a British national, very different case. And you know how I adore you.'

'Anyway, she doesn't seem to have a problem now,

said something about not needing one anymore.'

'I don't understand how. Her expiry date must be up by now. And from my enquiries, she wasn't going to be granted an extension.'

'She must have got a fake one. In which case she won't want publicity for herself or she'll get in trouble. But at the same time you don't want anybody knowing you had sex with a Brazilian cleaner who you knew no longer had a valid visa.'

Judge Stephenson nodded apprehensively, a fleeting image of his career careening off a cliff. He swallowed and looked to Linda for help. She duly obliged:

'What you need to do is go home and delete all the files on your computer. Then you need to contact Barbara and pay her off. I imagine she's pretty cheap. Probably just a few thousand – sure you can afford it, especially to avoid any scandal.'

'You're right, absolutely right, what would I ever do without you?'

The judge stood up to leave, kissing Linda on the cheek. Linda pouting:

'I'm a little short of money myself at the moment.'

'Of course, go and do a little shopping while I put the house in order. How much do you need?'

'Thousand?'

The judge whipped out his cheque book.

'In cash.'

The judge put the cheque book away.

'We'll stop at a cash machine. And I'll drop you at Harvey Nicks on the way – maybe get something lacy for later?'

After the judge gave her the money and went in search of Barbara, Linda called Barbara:

'Hey, how's it going sister?'

In the middle of choosing fake wedding rings, Barbara answered casually:

'Yea, is cool.'

'Just seeing if you've got in touch with the judge yet? Think you're on a winner there.'

'Oh well, am leaving it for moment.'

Linda caught her hesitation:

'You don't need the money anymore?'

Out of female loyalty, Barbara felt she owed Linda something, now that she had reverted to taking her money. But money was money and she could hardly say that it was Linda's she'd be taking:

'Yes I need, but I just wait for right time.'

'I really hope you're not going behind my back with Colin again.'

'With that cafetina? No way. Vinnie he's the one with brains.'

Vinnie, Linda quickly racking her brains. Colin's old mate from the cruise ships.

'Oh I've been meaning to get in touch with Vinnie for ages, got something of his sister's from when they visited us in Japan. Based up in North London now isn't he, don't know the address do you?'

Barbara didn't reply immediately. She didn't trust Linda but this was all too complicated and she did feel a bit bad going behind Linda's back. Vinnie would know what to do.

'Is called Blue Sky – Media Design, on the Holloway Road.'

'Barbara, you're a star. Now don't forget to get onto the judge. I'm sure he'll pay out.'

With relief, Barbara went back to choosing fake wedding rings. Vinnie could deal with Linda.

Clicking off the call, Linda looked up Blue Sky Media Design on her iPhone. She could do research same as Colin. The website was very pro, showing the company had some top clients. He was obviously on the rise. And all legit. So why was he getting messed up with Colin and Barbara? Okay, Barbara for her amazing assets obviously. And Colin must be out of misguided loyalty and friendship. So she'd need to put in an offer that topped that.

Linda already had a hair appointment booked. She had planned simply to have her roots dyed blonde as it was starting to show. Instead she had it dyed back to natural black and styled in a Japanese knot.

Next, Linda shopped for a suit. She wasn't sure how she'd look, but if you paid enough you could always look good. Just the right tightness around her pert bottom, the trouser suit was both professional and sexy. Sharp white shirt collar, at an angle over the top of her black jacket, one button of her shirt undone, jacket clasped around her waist by the middle button. It briefly reminded her of Colin's suit when they'd got married, but she quickly dispelled the memory. She blew a kiss to herself in the mirror. Gone was the blonde bombshell, replaced by a sophisticated black-haired businesswoman.

As Linda strutted into Blue Sky – Media Design, she remembered how Colin had eulogised Vinnie when they'd first met. Apparently a cool guy on the cruise ships. The way Colin had talked, he obviously looked up to him. Vinnie turned around from the pc he was working on and came out to greet her.

'How can I help you madam?'

Linda liked Vinnie's tone. Respectful without a trace of innuendo. The suit doing its job. It made a refreshing change from the act she'd been playing since god knows when, since she was sixteen probably.

'I have a business proposition through a mutual friend.'

Vinnie frowned, trying to work out which proposition and friend this was. Enjoying her role, Linda quizzed him:

'You are Vincent Gardener, the owner of this establishment?'

Vinnie nodded, it dawning on him:

'And you must be S.Y...Linda.'

'That's correct, but what was the first part?'

'Sorry, had a lot of names around my head recently. Come in.'

Vinnie lifted the counter flap for Linda to enter. Wow, she was good he thought. From Barbara's description and Colin's tales, he had her down as a bubbly blonde bombshell, sexy and conniving. But she'd had him fooled.

'Can I get you anything?'

'No thanks, this is strictly business.'

Vinnie nodded. He sat opposite her, looking her directly in the eye. He could do business. He could see why Colin had fallen for her. She was a great looking girl. And he could see how the scams had worked, Linda a natural actress. But he knew straight away there was going to be no playing around.

'So, how would you like to proceed?'

He could talk the talk too.

'Colin's initial plan failed miserably. I'm guessing he's come to you for a new one. I understand why you're helping Barbara. Breasts like hers, if I was a man, I'd be helping too. But I'm not sure why you're helping a fuck up like Colin.'

Vinnie squinted at Linda:

'How do you know I'm helping?'

'I know some new plan is afoot. Sooner or later I will find out what it is. Who do you think was the brains behind our scams?'

Vinnie didn't need to answer:

'So let me get this straight. You walk in here, large as life and expect me to explain Colin's plan of how he is going to get the money?'

'That's correct.'

'You're asking me to betray an old friend?'

'Is he really such a friend? We've been back nearly a year and I don't remember him getting in touch with you once, until he needed your help.'

Vinnie had joked about the same thing with Colin when he'd phoned up out of the blue. Linda had certainly struck a chord. The days on the cruise ships playing Colin's older brother were long gone. Not only did Vinnie owe Colin nothing, if anything it was the other way around. But still, his feelings either way were not part of business, and it was an easily read move by Linda.

'You think that is going to sway me?'

'No, that was just an observation. I think an offer of thirty percent will sway you. That's Colin's share.'

'You know if you offered him 50-50 he'd probably go for it and you could end all this.'

'No can do I'm afraid. It's a matter of principle now. He's brought it all on himself. I don't mind who gets the thirty per cent, but I worked very hard for that money. I want what's mine.'

Vinnie rubbed his head:

'Let me guess, there's some blackmail here. If I don't

go along with you, you'll be going along to the police about Barbara's visa. But they'll find me clean.'

'No blackmail. It's a straight up deal Vincent. Take it or leave it. You've just got to ask yourself, knowing Colin as you do – who do you think has the bigger balls? Who do you see coming out of this with the money?'

Vinnie nodding, a slight smile on his lips, you had to hand it to her:

'I see your point…'

Linda offered her hand:

'Do we have a deal or not?'

CHAPTER 15

In the Piccadilly branch of HSBC, Colin and Barbara were sitting in the manager's office upstairs, Colin explaining to the manager:

'I know it's an unusual request, but she's got her heart set on it. My wife and I always planned on retiring to sunnier climes. Bit young I know to be thinking about that, but after living in Rio it's hard not to want to go back. It's where we met of course, at the carnival, my future wife the prettiest flamingo on parade. Fell in love at first sight.'

Colin believing his spiel, some of the feelings even initially true, just to do with Linda rather than Barbara. If she could see him now, he'd show her how to act. Barbara sat there with a smile plastered on her face as Colin continued:

'And with her great uncle's beach house coming on the market, we just had to snap it up. Thing is, it's a quick-fire cash sale. All above board of course, but the present owner will accept a lot less this way. I said it's almost all of our savings but she insists, so what am I supposed to do?'

Barbara rolled her eyes to the manager, turned to Colin:

'Come on darling, he not interested in our story. We need to be hurry soon or the house will go.'

It wasn't difficult for Barbara to play the part of

impatient wife, apart from the use of the word 'darling'. The bank manager wasn't interested in why they needed the money, but he was interested in how they had it:

'For security reasons, I have to ask you some questions. Looking at your account and personal details, your credit ratings are fine. However, looking up your transactions I have noticed that approximately eighteen thousand pounds started going into your account six months ago every month. May I ask if this is from your work?'

Expecting this, Colin smiled:

'Have you heard of Crosswell tea cakes?'

'Yes, naturally.'

'My Grandfather was the original owner before it changed hands. For a long time there has been a legal battle going on about the name, it's all been kept very low key, out of the press, but six months ago, an agreement was finally settled and the money paid to us in installments.'

'I see, I did wonder about the name. In that case, if I can just see some ID?'

Colin handed over his driving licence. Barbara did likewise, the difference being that hers was fake. It had her picture but Linda's name. The bank manager looked at the photographs and at the two of them, handing them back:

'Ok, that's fine. If I could have your bank cards please.'

The two of them handed over their cards, Barbara's again fake. If the bank manager tried to put it in a machine it wouldn't work, but all he wanted was to check their signatures as he slid over a piece of paper:

'I need you both to sign here.'

They both signed, Colin first with his real signature. Barbara took the pen and with a swirl, signed her newly learnt 'Linda Crosswell'. With a satisfied smile, she handed the pen and paper over to the manager. He examined the two signatures, comparing them to the back of their bank cards. Again, everything was in order. It did seem strange to him that a couple wanted to take out nearly the whole of their savings in one go, but it was their choice to do so and he'd checked everything. He got onto the internal phone:

'Sandra, could you bring in the money for the Crosswell account please.'

Sandra, in her bank assistant white shirt and grey trousers, brought in a metal container. She opened it and counted out the money, two hundred thousand pounds, in one hundred pound notes. Once it was all counted, the bank manager looked toward Colin, who nodded back. The money was transferred to the briefcase, and hands shaken.

Out of the bank, Colin sighed with relief while Barbara lit up. Barbara thinking Vinnie's plan had worked a treat, and he knew how to give a girl a good time too. No longer needing to act their roles, they walked in silence to Leicester Square tube station and got the Piccadilly Line up to Holloway Road.

They had pulled it off, thought Colin. The first part had gone to plan. He almost felt like sending a text to Linda: 'check the account'. But then she'd call the police and him and Barbara would be done for impersonation. No, she couldn't ever know. Though he couldn't help smiling at the thought of Linda on one of her shopping sprees only to find her card was declined.

Linda walked into Starbucks off Piccadilly where she'd arranged to meet James Littlewood, Linda armed with a disc of Barbara and the judge. The judge's mention of Littlewood was just confirmation to Linda that she had chosen the right journalist. She'd seen his article the day before in the Evening Standard and elicited from the judge that he was a regular down at the courts.

Littlewood was already sat, working on his laptop, coffee by the side. Linda stood over him,

'James Littlewood?'

'That's me. I take it you're who phoned me earlier.'

As her answer, Linda sat opposite him. He leant back, said:

'I hope it's worth it. I'm a busy man. I've a deadline coming up in the next hour.'

'How about this, Judge Stephenson having sex with his Brazilian cleaner, who is here on an illegal visa.'

'And what are you, an estranged girlfriend?'

'No, I'm Ms. Anonymous.'

'And you have proof of this?'

'Have a look for yourself.'

Linda handed over the disc to the journalist. He took it, put it in his laptop and sat back to watch. His eyebrows raised:

'She should be on page three of The Sun.'

Littlewood stopped the film, looked across at Linda:

'Okay, pretty good stuff, but how do I know it's not his girlfriend?'

'You're the journalist, do some research. But do you think a girl with her assets would be having sex with a bearded man in his forties if there wasn't something to gain?'

'You sure I can't fit you into the story somewhere?'

'I'm sure. Now what about the price?'

'It's good I'll give you that, might be able to persuade my editor to go as high as two thousand.'

'Cut the shit, I'm in a hurry, five thousand or one of your competitors gets it.'

'Four thousand.'

'Four thousand five hundred or you can admire my arse as I leave and get on the phone to someone else.'

'Okay, okay, four thousand five hundred it is.'

After leaving Littlewood to get working on the story of the judge and his illegal cleaner lover, Linda went into a public phone box. The last time she'd been into one of those was when she was a little girl, but she didn't want to be traced by her mobile number.

After a several minutes wait of soft music interrupted

by announcements stating that an advisor would shortly be with her, finally someone answered:

'Immigration hotline. Tracey speaking. How can I help?'

'Hi, I'd like to report someone being here illegally. The name is Barbara De Santos, address Flat 3, 21 Vorley Road, Archway N1.'

'Can I have your contact number?'

'No, you can't. She is not only here illegally but also has a fake visa. I think someone should get onto it in a hurry before she moves on.'

Linda put the phone down.

When Colin and Barbara entered Blue Sky - Media Design, Vinnie was just handing over a print-out to a man in a suit with a briefcase. Colin and Barbara waited as if they were customers. With the other customer satisfied, he left and Vinnie turned to Colin and Barbara:

'How can I help?'

Colin placed the suitcase on the counter:

'Yes, I have two hundred thousand pounds in here. I wonder if you could hold onto it for me.'

'I think you'd better come into my office.'

The three of them went into the back. With the suitcase full of money on one of the chairs, Vinnie took charge:

'Okay, Barbara as promised, here is your share for helping. Ten thousand sound okay?'

It sounded more than okay, Barbara accepting the

money and stuffing it into her handbag. Vinnie gave instructions:

'Now go and put it somewhere safe at home.'

Barbara raised her eyebrows suggestively, turned and swayed out of the store. Colin turned to Vinnie:

'Look mate, you've been such a great help, you deserve a share. Just take whatever you think is right.'

'Hey, what are mates for. But look, are you going to take this? You can't walk around London with this much cash on you - a briefcase full of money? Come on. Here's what we'll do, my last favour, I'll leave the money for you in a locker at Heathrow with the key at the Thai Air desk. How does that sound?'

'Sounds like a plan. I better get down to Tooting, get my stuff. Mate, I owe you big time.'

'You get settled in Thailand, you're paying for my holiday over.'

'Be like the old days – girls, drink and drugs.'

Vinnie cracked a smile, put out a muscled arm – embracing Colin in a man hug before slapping him on the shoulder:

'Get out of here.'

Judge Stephenson pulled his bright yellow VW into the parking space by the side of his house in Kingsley Place. He picked his briefcase off the passenger seat. All it contained was his wig. He was eagerly anticipating Linda's sexual punishment for discovering his secret filming. She hadn't seemed upset by it at all. Barbara had been pretty good with her enormous breasts, but Linda was tougher, sexier, brighter.

He'd deleted all his wonderful home movies before returning to work, sad to see them go but knowing it was a necessity. He'd tried ringing Barbara to pay her off as Linda had suggested but she hadn't answered her phone. He'd almost popped around to her hovel in Archway but had decided it could wait until morning. Especially when he had Linda's spanking to look forward to, the judge barely able to contain his excitement.

He bleeped the car to lock and started off for his front door. Before he reached it however, he heard a familiar voice:

'Judge Stephenson, can we have a word?'

Judge Stephenson turned to find James Littlewood walking up to him, dictaphone in his hand. A photographer was with him. The judge had seen James only that morning outside court, and it was unusual for the papers to actually come to his house, but he was always willing to give a quote. With a satisfied smile, he said:

'Forgot to ask a question this morning James?'

'This is for a different story. I wonder judge if we could have your views on immigrants staying here on illegal visas?'

'But what has that got to do with the Stockwell Three?'

'Nothing, nothing at all Judge Stephenson.'

'I don't understand…'

'Judge Stephenson, is it true that you had sex with your Brazilian cleaner in return for promising her a visa?'

'I'm sorry I don't know what you are talking about.'

'The film we have obtained of the two of you is pretty conclusive. Are you denying that you had sex with her?'

'I…' the Judge stammered, confused, 'no comment.'

The judge didn't like the way these questions were going at all, turning hurriedly to his front door, desperately unlocking it as James Littlewood fired his next question:

'Do you not think Judge Stephenson that it is hypocritical for a judge of your stature…'

Judge Stephenson got the door open, slamming it shut behind him as the camera flashed.

It was quiet inside the house as he stayed leaning against the door, the dread setting in.

Sure enough, less than a minute later his mobile rang. He looked at the caller – Irvin Wilkinson, the judge supreme, the only person he could really call his boss. Judge Stephenson guessed Irvin wasn't calling to congratulate him for his post Stockwell Three interview.

He turned the phone off. He opened his briefcase with wig inside, took it out. He put it on and went to the bathroom, looked in the mirror. He didn't imagine he'd be seeing himself in it any longer.

Barbara had just got of the shower, towel wrapped around

her, feeling that everything was going pretty well. In one day, she'd got a year's salary. And she still planned on getting more money from the judge. At this rate she really would be able to buy a beach house. Maybe even set up her own secretarial business. Sure, Colin was getting a lot more, but that was his anyway. She wasn't greedy, just wanted what should be hers. She didn't give much thought to Linda losing out. Sure, for a moment they'd been sisters, but you had to adapt, go with the flow, and the flow as far as she was concerned, was with Vinnie. Fuck the judge, she didn't need him anymore. She had her visa stamped in her passport and money enough for the next year whether she worked or not.

And she didn't think she'd be much longer in the room she was in. She was sure with a bit of persuading she could get Vinnie to let her move in with him. He was a real man, not like the judge with his little routine and secret camera and broken promises, or like Colin, so weak, he made his own wife sleep with other men because he couldn't get it up. Vinnie had grande testiculos and grande cranio.

That was what she was thinking when she heard a knock on the door. Without thinking, she opened it. Two men in cheap grey suits were standing there, one in front of the other. The one in front said:

'Ms. De Santos?'

She was instantly suspicious, but it didn't stop her from hesitantly answering:

'Yes.'

The man who'd asked the question held up an ID card:

'Immigration. May we come in?'

Barbara had to think quickly. If she shut the door on them, it would be obvious she had something to hide. They couldn't possibly know so quickly that she had gone past her expiry date and gained a fake visa, could they? She played it cool:

'Is important? As you see, I am getting dressed.'

'Ms De Santos, we believe your visa to stay here expired a considerable time ago'

She had no choice but to bluff:

'Is some mistake. I get new visa.'

'May we see it?'

Barbara sighed dramatically as she let the two men into her small room. She got her passport out of her handbag, flipped to the page with the new visa stamped in, displayed the page, not actually handing it over. The immigration man put his hand out:

'May I?'

'Of course. See, is new visa. I am here one year, so get extension with work. Maybe some mistake on system, doesn't show up.'

Barbara was acting as casually as possible, whilst at the same time, manoeuvring her body to display the curves of her breasts. A girl had to use her assets, as Linda had said. But the immigration officer didn't seem to notice them:

'Ms De Santos, you may well be in bigger trouble than at first thought.'

'Sorry?'

'Where did you obtain this visa?'

'From immigration office, you know down in Croydon.'

'Ms De Santos, we know that you were not granted an extension of your visa. Which means that this is a copy.'

'I can't believe. The man in Croydon, he put stamp there, say it is all official.'

'Please, Ms De Santos…'

'I know what this is about. The man I saw, he asked me, do I want to go with him, you know, for sex. I say no, I just need my visa thank you. And because I refuse him, he don't process my visa on system. Typical. You know I see in newspapers, but I don't believe is actually possible.'

Barbara was shaking her head in disbelief. The immigration official was unmoved:

'Ms De Santos, if you stay beyond your visa expiry date, you simply get deported. Purchasing a fake visa however is a criminal offence and will lead to a court hearing with the likely result that you will be imprisoned.'

It didn't matter what country you were in, it was always the same. With a tired sigh, Barbara accidentally on purpose let go of her towel, displaying her whole body, breasts prominent. She looked at both of the men:

'Okay, who wants to go first?'

The assistant's eyes were wide open, fixated on

Barbara's breasts. The main official however, kept his eyes focused on Barbara's:

'Ms De Santos, for your own benefit I will ignore the fact that you have just tried to bribe two immigration officials. What could help you instead is telling us who you got this fake visa from.'

Barbara picked up the towel. Not bothering to wrap it around her voluptuous body, she shrugged. Picking up a cigarette, she said:

'I tell you, how is going to help me?'

'As I said earlier, it is the difference between simply being deported back to Brazil or going down the road to Holloway Prison.'

Maybe it was time to go back to Brazil, thought Barbara. Cut losses. She had ten thousand pounds. Who wanted to be in Britain anyway? Always bloody raining. And the men were nearly all weak, all apart from Vinnie, but then he was probably the one who had shopped her. It could only have been him or Colin. But naming Colin wasn't going to get her out of her predicament. Oh well, it had been good with Vinnie while it had lasted.

'You have a paper and pen?'

'Yes, why?'

'You gonna need it for the story I got.'

CHAPTER 16

When Colin first walked down Totterdown Street, he saw that the lights in the flat were on, so backtracked and went into the local pub on the corner - The World's End. It wasn't eleven yet. He could wait. SYBU was in the flat that was the important thing.

He also needed to pep talk himself. Was he really going to kill Linda? When he'd said it to Vinnie, his old mate had dismissed it, insinuated he didn't have it in him. Colin hadn't mentioned it again. But the intention had taken root, and the more he thought about it the more it seemed the only way. He just needed a quick drink that was all.

The pub smelt of the day before's sick, appropriate thought Colin, for the world ending. He ordered a pint of London Pride. He was feeling bitter. And he was about to restore his pride, so it seemed the right drink. He felt like something stronger but needed the drink to last and didn't want to sit there getting plastered on whiskeys or whatever.

He was still in the smart shirt and trousers he'd bought on Upper Street earlier in the afternoon, looking out of place in The World's End on the corner of Totterdown Street, Tooting Broadway, full as it was with hardened drinkers, locals in paint-stained work clothes. In the inside of his new jacket pocket was the plane ticket to Thailand.

After leaving Vinnie with the briefcase of money, he'd gone directly down to the Thai Air flight office in Piccadilly. The girl there had asked him a couple of times if he was sure that this was the flight he wanted, it probably looking a bit strange someone coming in to book a long distance flight for the next morning and paying in cash.

Knowing that the flight to Thailand was a one-way ticket with no option of coming back, Colin had thought about calling his parents, but then thought, why? Tickets and call, or non-call, to parents ticked, the only other thing he needed was a change of clothes and some of his stuff, which he'd get from the flat.

Colin finished his first pint, looked at his mobile to check the time. Still wasn't quite eleven, she probably wouldn't be asleep yet. He ordered another pint. When he wasn't drinking it, he was staring into it. Going over and over what he'd set himself to do.

He could always back out, simply run with the money. But she deserved what she was about to get, Colin building up his bitter feelings as he re-ran every humiliation Linda had laid on him – throwing her wedding ring in the rubbish, fucking the judge while they were still married, spreading lies about his manhood. What was he going to do, not carry it out? Besides, she was so clever, she'd probably find a way of tracking him down to Thailand.

He imagined talking to Vinnie in the future, sitting in a bar overlooking the beach in Thailand:

'You see you don't understand. It's easy to look at it from an outside point of view. But what was I supposed to do, let her laugh at me the rest of her life. She'd humiliated me, fucked another man while she was still married to me, made me sleep in another room, constantly mocked me, tried to take all the money, tried to have me put in jail.'

'But you got the money didn't you?'

'Yea, but it wasn't enough. She was still laughing at me. I had to make it so that she could never laugh again.'

Colin came out of his reverie, looked at his mobile. It was past eleven. In the past the pub would already have rang the bell for last orders. Kind of pub like The World's End, it probably wouldn't have mattered anyway, just do a lock in. But with the new licensing laws, it was possible for pubs to be open all hours. He took his empty glass to the bar, ordered a whiskey, straight, downed it for the hit, turned and left the pub.

He felt wired, a cocaine type rush in his brain, playing the Stone Roses in his mind, light footed from the beer and no food all day, but clear sighted. The light in the flat was off. The cinematic movement he pictured himself in drove him onwards as he strode to the building, up the stairs, opening the door.

He didn't care if she heard him come in. He knew she wasn't scared of him. He walked through the living room, picking up the pillow from the sofa on his way, pushed open the bed- room door. Linda didn't move. She had no fear of him at all, never thought he would be capable of hurting her, thought she was above him.

Colin stood for a few seconds, letting his eyes adjust. He saw the outline of her head and pictured that mouth that could laugh so easily but also curl in hate. It almost came to him which actress she reminded him of. The name still escaped him, but he knew she nearly always ended up dead by the end of the film. He couldn't turn back. Now or never, he thought.

Colin walked over to the bed, then leapt onto it, simultaneously pinning Linda's body under the covers with his weight and pressing the pillow down on her face. Except it was too soft to be Linda's body. He instantly shot his arm under the covers, his hand pressing into pillows. He jumped up, snapped on the light. The bedroom was a mess, drawers pulled out, clothes scattered on the carpet as if there had been a huge struggle. Colin's eyes drifted to the pillow he thought had been Linda's head. It was streaked with blood.

What was going on? Something was very wrong here. He hadn't killed Linda, but it sure looked like he already had. Either something bad had happened in the flat or Linda had staged it. Either way, he had to get out. The distant sound of a police siren set his legs in motion, Colin scarpering out of the flat.

Vinnie frowned and put down his cup of tea. Someone was incessantly knocking on the metal shutters outside the front door. Reluctantly he made his way downstairs.

The metal shutters that protected the glass door and windows were still being banged on. As Vinnie pressed the button to haul up the shutter, he called out:

'Okay, okay, keep your hair on.'

The metal shutters rose to show a tall man in a crumpled suit, accompanied by two policemen. Vinnie guessed the tall man must be plain clothes, detective maybe, especially when the man said:

'Vincent Gardener?'

'That's me.'

'I'm Detective Friend. May I come in?'

'Got any ID?'

Detective Friend flashed his ID. Vinnie though was holding his ground:

'Mind if I take a closer look?'

Detective Friend held the ID up, Vinnie examining it. Vinnie gave a nod, mouth down-turned in acceptance:

'Can't be too careful. People try all sorts of scams, dress up as policemen so that they can get into someone's place, then rob them. Come in.'

Vinnie held the door open. Detective Friend and his two officers entered. Vinnie asked:

'So how can I help you detective Friend? Is that for real – Friend, that's your surname?'

'Well seeing as you've so kindly invited us into your premises, you've saved us the job of having to request a warrant to search the property. And yes, that is my real surname.'

'Hey, that was good, you got me with that little trick. I don't know what it is you're hoping to find here, but hey, be my guest, I've got nothing to hide.'

Detective Friend gestured for the two policemen to go through to Vincent's work area. Detective Friend held up Barbara's passport, displaying the page with the fake visa. After her story, she'd been hauled down to the local police station. It had taken until eleven o'clock at night to check out her story. Detective Richard Friend was on evening duty so got assigned the case. He asked:

'You know anything about this?'

'No, what is it?'

'It's a fake visa. The woman, Barbara De Santos, Brazilian, brown skin, blue eyes, size thirty six D, I think you'd remember her if you saw her, she seems to know you.'

'Yea, she was here, but I didn't do that visa.'

'That's funny, because she said you did.'

'What is this, he's black so he's got to be guilty? Look I know it's all in the news about those kids from Stockwell, but it doesn't mean every black man is raping some girl. See those kids, their problem is that they don't know who they are. They all think they're in some gangsta rap video, imagining that they can do the same. Me, I know who I am, don't pretend to be anything else. Sure, I'm black, but I was born right around the corner. Yea, I travelled around a bit, but now I'm back and trying to make a living with my own business.'

175

'And the point is?'

'Point is, Barbara came here and as you've noticed yourself, she's got some assets. She offered and I didn't refuse. Then she tried to blackmail me.'

Detective Friend found it hard to believe:

'She tried to blackmail you?'

'Yea, I couldn't believe it either. I said you should never blackmail a black male – do you like that?'

Detective Friend ignored Vinnie's attempt at humour:

'I'd like to know how it is that she tried to blackmail you.'

'Said if I didn't help her make a fake visa, she'd say I raped her.'

'That's not what she said to us. What she told us was that you made the visa for her. That's what interests me.'

'So a girl allegedly being raped doesn't interest you?'

Detective Friend gave Vinnie a stern look. Vinnie smiled:

'Okay, okay. Look, can I get you guys a cup of tea or something while you're looking for whatever it is you're looking for?'

Before Detective Friend could answer, one of the two police- men came over, handing over an ID card. Detective Friend looked at the card, then showed it to Vinnie:

'What's this, another fake ID card?'

'No, that's Colin's.'

'Who's Colin?'

'Works for me.'

'Look Vincent…'

'Vinnie will do.'

'Vinnie, Barbara is saying that you made this visa. You've admitted she was here. You've got the facilities to do it, we take everything away, get it tested, we'll find out what you've been doing. You're hiding something. You don't come clean, you're going to take the rap, one way or the other.'

'You saying that you can fake the evidence?'

'I'm saying you should tell me what you know.'

'Look, Colin's a mate.'

'Withholding evidence is a crime as I'm sure you know.'

'Ok, look I'm just trying to protect him, but maybe it's better this way, stop him from doing anything stupid, if he hasn't already. Colin and me go way back – we did the cruise ships together. Anyway he stopped off in Japan for a year or so, then had some whirlwind romance, got married in Vegas.'

'With a Japanese girl?'

'No, a Manchester girl. Anyway, he gets back in London, he needs a job. I've set up my own business, so I give him hours occasionally when I need help.'

'He on your books?'

'It was cash in hand, I was helping him out, but come on you're not going to do me for not putting it down for tax are you? He was going through a really rough time, his wife had started sleeping with some judge, in fact I think it was the one in charge of the Stockwell Three case.

'Barbara also had something to do with the judge, his cleaner or something and she was upset because he'd promised her a visa but went back on the promise. So somehow Colin and Barbara got together, don't ask me how. She came in here one time, asked me to do the visa for her, in exchange for what I'm sure you can guess.

'I refused to help, you think I want to lose this business I just set up? But I did take up what was on offer, I mean who wouldn't? I advised Colin not to help her either, but he obviously did. I'm not here twenty four seven, he could easily have used the facilities one afternoon.

'I think they also had some crazy plan to blackmail the judge and he even mentioned killing Linda – that's his wife. I thought he was all talk, but...'

Detective Friend looked into Vinnie's eyes, trying to determine how much of what he'd said was true. He could easily be lying but it was true that it would be stupid to risk his business for someone as unreliable as Barbara, who quite obviously was trying to save her own skin whatever way was possible. Vinnie had stayed cool throughout, though that could also be a façade. Only one way to find out:

'Ok, let's check out some of this story.'

Detective Friend got on his mobile:

'Hey it's Richard, have you still got her there? Ok, ask

her if she knows a Colin…'

The detective looked to Vinnie for the surname, Vinnie providing it:

'Crosswell, like the teacakes.'

Detective Friend continuing into his mobile:

'Crosswell…yea, like the teacakes. Also find out if she knows about his wife, Linda…'

The detective looked to Vinnie again, the surname coming:

'Collins – like his name with an 's' at the end.'

Detective Friend repeating:

'Collins…yea like his name with an 's' at the end. And find out if Barbara was previously sleeping with Judge Stephenson…yea, who did the Stockwell Three case, but was jilted for Colin Croswell's wife. Got all that? Ok, when you get any answers get back to me.'

Detective Friend got off his mobile. Vinnie looked to the detective and two policemen:

'So do you want a cup of tea? Can't offer you anything else as I don't drink alcohol. And got no biscuits to go with it I'm afraid.'

The two policemen looked hopefully at the detective, but he snuffed out their hope:

'We're alright thanks.'

The mobile rang. Detective Friend answered:

'What have you got?'

He listened for a few minutes, then said:

'Yea? Okay…alright, cheers.'

He beeped off his mobile, looked at Vinnie:

'She's naming whoever she can, though her version still doesn't match yours. But something else seems to corroborate what you say. The press have got hold of the story. She was trying to blackmail the judge, they even have a film of the two of them together. Going to be all over the papers tomorrow.'

Vinnie gave a shrug, one hand rubbing the back of his bald head as he said:

'Sorry I'm not your man.'

'Doesn't mean we've finished questioning you, but for now we'll take your word on things. Now what about this Colin Crosswell – you think he's serious about killing his wife?'

'I really don't know, but the way things are panning out with fake visas and blackmail, I wouldn't rule it out. And after that he was planning to get a plane to Thailand.'

'Got an address?'

'21 Totterdown Street, flat 3 I think. It's in Tooting Broadway end of the Northern Line.'

'I know where Tooting Broadway is. We'll be in touch if we need a statement from you.'

'No problem.'

The detective and two policemen left in a hurry, Vinnie lowering the metal shutters behind them.

Vinnie nodded to himself as he clicked off the lights and went upstairs to his flat. It was all working out pretty good. He'd guessed that Linda would put Barbara and the judge in it and was sure that once Barbara was in it she'd put anyone else in it if it helped her. With or without a search warrant, Vinnie was always pre-prepped for any police visit. All the machines were clean, the fake passports were in a secret safe in his flat, and his flat was in fact under a different name so would require a separate warrant.

Upstairs, he looked down at the two briefcases by the side of the sofa.

Linda held out a cup of tea to Vinnie:

'I made you a fresh cup.'

Vinnie took a gulp, nodded in approval:

'Good northern cup of tea. And thanks for letting me know you called immigration on Barbara.'

'I knew you'd deal with it. Besides it had to seem real for the police.'

Linda rubbed the plaster on her finger, sore where she'd held the hot cup. She had enjoyed tearing her old bedroom apart, but giving blood hadn't been such a nice task. Looking away and grimacing, she'd pressed the edge of a sharp kitchen knife into her finger over the pillow. Letting it bleed, she'd wiped it on the pillow several times to leave a trail, before sticking on a plaster.

Linda looked at her new passport:

'You did a good job.'

'Cheers.'

'I've divided the money up. You want to check?'

Vinnie gulped down the rest of his tea. You bet he wanted to check. Until Linda was out of the door and he had his share, he didn't trust her an inch. But strangely, he suddenly felt tired. Man, his eyelids were even starting to close. And he was having trouble getting his words out. Had he just said any of that out loud? He tried to formulate a question, but his jaw seemed to pause. Linda was all blurred in front of him. He reached out for the edge of the sofa but was no longer sure where it was. Vinnie crashed onto the floor, the room spinning, his breathing shallow.

Linda pursed her lips. Pity, she genuinely liked Vinnie, but in this world you couldn't trust anyone. Hopefully the dose would just knock him out for awhile rather than kill him. She pocketed the passport. Together with the one she had from the judge, she'd easily be able to leave a false trail. She checked her flight tickets and smiled. Ironic that she'd be getting on the same plane that Colin had booked onto. She picked up the suitcase with all the money in and sashayed out.

Colin had to wait for the tube to arrive, the late night services running at longer intervals. At least he would never have to get on the Northern Line again.

At Leicester Square he changed onto the Piccadilly Line, getting a Westbound to Heathrow. He would be there about one in the morning. The flight was at five, so he'd have a few hours to kill, but that was ok. For a start he had to collect the money. He looked at his mobile. He hadn't had a message from Vinnie confirming the locker key was at the Thai Air desk so that he could pick up his case, but then there was no signal of course on the underground. He had time for the message to come through.

With the adrenalin winding down, music was no longer in his head, replaced by the mundane rattling of the tube journey. He picked up a crumpled Metro which had been read and discarded by who knew how many people that day.

The Stockwell Three case was still big news, politicians divided about the judge's stance, whether it had been right to make the case so public.

The tube was rattling along above ground now, past Northfields, looming towards Heathrow. Colin was coming down, doubts creeping in, dread forming. There was still no message from Vinnie on his mobile.

Looking out of the tube windows, Colin saw cherry trees in blossom, the pink blossom lit up strangely by orange street lamps. It was the first time he'd noticed it was spring, first time come to think of it he'd noticed which season it was since...spring time in Tokyo one year ago. The summer had passed in the heat of passion, autumn had bypassed him as they sat getting depressed back in London, winter had passed by in a flurry of scams...

The tube went back underground, shaking to a stop at the terminals. Colin almost felt like simply staying on, letting the tube take him back into the city. But he forced himself to get off.

He let the escalators take him up a level, remembering how he used to stand one step below Linda so they could be the same height. On a stand, a man was unpacking the early morning editions of the papers. Colin saw the headline – "Stockwell Three Judge in sex for visa scandal with illegal cleaner."

Colin knew. He knew he wasn't getting on a plane, knew that Vinnie wasn't going to send any message, that Linda had somehow set him up for a fall. And when he turned and saw a man in a crumpled suit accompanied by two policemen, looking at him from the other side of the ticket barrier, he knew they were waiting for him.

He didn't know that the man in the crumpled suit was Detective Friend or that the local police in Tooting had got to his flat ten minutes after he'd left. But he knew that there was no way out.

Colin didn't move, his eyes glazing over. He no longer saw the policemen approaching him. He saw Linda's mouth curled in a mocking sneer.

The detective, flanked on both sides by uniformed policemen, came back into focus, close up now, his mouth opening in slow motion:

'Colin Crosswell, you are under arrest for the murder of your wife, Linda Collins.'

Colin wanted to press 'stop'. But it wasn't a film, it was his life. And even if he could – 'play from start' or 'resume from previous scene'?

EPILOGUE

Feeling sick before he'd even eaten, Colin reached for the postcard that arrived with the breakfast tray. In the foreground, palm trees dotted the sweep of beach. In the background, a small island jutted out of the clear sea.

He knew it was no use, but turned the card over. Blank apart from his name and prison address. He Blu-Tacked it to the cell wall, number fifty two in the grid of postcards. There was no point in getting it tested for fingerprints to prove Linda was still alive. In court, they'd tried to use Vinnie's testament to prove Linda had staged her own death – Vinnie regaining consciousness. But with no concrete evidence, Vinnie had gone down as well for forgery.

At least the cards marked the passing of time. A year now. Colin stood still in the middle of his cell, the fifty two postcards of sunlit beaches in Thailand glaring at him. Colin's eyes glazed over as he envisaged Linda lounged on a recliner, a young Thai guy massaging her feet while another held out a set of postcards. He saw her smile as she pointed one out, her lips ready to sneer. Colin blinked away the vision, tried to make sense of his situation:

Thought I got it right – do the crime first, then go on the run. Maybe there is no right way around…

THE END

Also by CAL SMYTH:

The Final Mile

Ryan Morgan is a good guy, a family man who runs his own business and lives by the rules. But when his business is liquidated, his house repossessed and his wife leaves him, Ryan starts to question the system. For years, the rich have ripped us off. It's time someone made them pay.

Seeking payback, Ryan treks cross-country through a broken Britain menaced by an economic crisis. With nothing left to lose, Ryan cuts a brutally sweet swathe through the murky greed and corruption of bankers, CEO's and politicians whose skewered morals and hypocrisy have crippled a nation

A stunning tale of morality and justice in which a simple, honest man is transformed into a killer, The Final Mile depicts a moral turnaround in the vein of TV's Breaking Bad. A story ripped from the headlines of tomorrow's newspapers. A biting social commentary of both the jobless hordes and the glitzy, gold-plated world of dirty deals and fat cat cronyism. A resonant wish-fulfilment thriller that is cinematic and sparse genre writing at its very best.

With nods to Richard Stark, Elmore Leonard and George Pelecanos, Cal Smyth has written a tale of revenge that challenges and entertains in equal measure: a blazing read that burns off the page, righteous indignation rippling through every heart-stopping moment...

Read the first few thrilling pages now...

Chapter 1

The explosion ripped through the armed vehicle, vibrated along the ground and threw Ryan backwards off his feet. Heavy in his bomb disposal suit, it felt like he was in slow motion as he forced himself back up.

He'd spotted the wires in the road and had immediately called for the vehicles to halt while he checked them out, but something had already set off the first bomb.

He turned away from the shards of metal and body parts. If anybody was still alive, it was up to the other guys to save them. His job was to disarm the gravel-covered bomb in front of the remaining vehicle.

Inside the vehicle was the fuckwit of a general who had made them take this route. The men had warned him that it was insurgent territory and hadn't been properly cleared. The idiot had ignored them. But there was no time to think about that. What Ryan had to focus on was de-wiring the explosive.

The vehicle couldn't go backwards because it was blocked by the blown up vehicle. For all of them, the only way out was forwards. That couldn't happen unless Ryan disarmed the bomb. And until then, they were sitting ducks for any snipers. Ryan knew the rest of the unit were covering his back as best they could but they could only do it for so long.

He stepped cautiously to the bomb poking out of the loose ground and examined the wiring. He had to get this right. Sweat dripped into his eyes.

Ryan blinked away the memory of his time in Kuwait. He had to focus. The footfalls were echoing his own, right behind him, breath on the back of his neck.

He forced his tired legs to move faster as he heard the footfalls close in behind him. Sweat glistened in the greying stubble of his closely cropped hair, drips stinging his eyes and making him squint in the sunlight. He could hear his breathing getting deeper and evened it out while pumping his legs and arms, ignoring the ache in his thigh muscles. He didn't take in the crowd to the side, but he heard the cries go up.

Ryan pushed through the pain, put in a final surge and tore through the tape at the finishing line.

Bent over as he regained his breath, Ryan was joined by Evan. The two men breathed heavily in tandem as they stood in similar positions. Evan looked across at his old school friend:

'One day I'll catch you.'

Ryan met Evan's eyes and gave a weary nod:

'Maybe next time.'

Back in senior school the two of them had been cross-country champions several years in a row, always finishing in the same positions in the Swansea interschool races – Ryan first, Evan second.

Their competitiveness hadn't ruined their friendship, but later they'd gone their separate ways – or Ryan had, into the armed forces for ten years while Evan worked his way up to DCI in the local police force. Ryan had been back in Swansea for twenty years now. They never met socially, though they always said they would. But they always met up once a year at the race.

It wasn't that Ryan had to beat Evan, just that if he was going to run in a race then he was in it to win it. He was in great shape for his fifty years, partly down to his genetic make-up and partly due to learnt behaviour – habits that were entrenched even before he joined the army. Not just his daily run, but his morning routine for the last thirty four years of pull-ups, sit-ups and press-ups.

Six foot two and wiry, Ryan's arms dangled when he strode places, his limber fingers ideal for playing guitar, though he'd never picked one up. His handsome face never betrayed much emotion, but his startling blue eyes were always alert - Ryan was never able to switch off. When he laughed or was pained, the lines around his eyes would crease up; that was the giveaway.

Right now, his eyes squinted from the glare of the mid-morning sun and took in his wife. She smiled at him across a table outside Verdi's, the seafront café. Sandra was looking at him with her calm expression, but she had a slight frown and she was smiling out of the side of her mouth, something she always did when she felt nervous. She was talking to a guy with designer sunglasses, pushed up in his precisely parted hair, the man with an untouched coffee in front of him. Swansea was such a small city, thought Ryan as he recognised the man. It was Huw, his bank manager.

Sandra said something to Huw before walking over to Ryan and Evan, a bottle of water in each hand, one for both men. She was wearing a skirt today, a black one that ended a few inches above her knees, and a pale white sleeveless blouse. Ryan liked the skirt a lot and he liked how she moved in it.

Sandra smiled as she reached the two men, shook her head as she coolly appraised the state of both Ryan and Evan:

'It's supposed to be a run for charity, not a race to the death.'

Ryan shrugged as he took a bottle of water, nimbly unscrewing the cap. He gulped the water down, his Adam's apple bobbing as the water gushed down his throat. Evan smiled as he took his bottle:

'Maybe you can tell your husband to be charitable and let me win one year.'

Ryan stopped drinking. He'd always been able to focus completely on the task in hand, but he'd let his mind wander back to memories of Kuwait and had nearly let Evan in this time.

Sandra turned to Ryan and kissed him on the lips. As ever, she looked fantastic and much younger than forty nine. She wasn't a fitness fanatic, but she looked after herself – zumba on Tuesday nights, swimming Thursday mornings. Monthly hair and beauty treatments, a holiday somewhere hot at least once a year.

She didn't hide her age through any artificial means, apart from dying her hair and using moisturisers, but which woman didn't? Ryan was staring at Sandra's profile: head slightly lowered, her dark hair falling past her shoulder, bare in the sleeveless blouse with a bra strap exposed. No doubt the bra was some kind of fashionable brand. Ryan wouldn't know what as he left that kind of thing to her. He'd once bought her underwear from La Senza as an anniversary gift, but only after she'd told him where to go and what to get. He'd been so flustered in the shop, he never did it again. The whole chain had since closed down anyway.

Ryan didn't tell her how good she looked, but was pretty sure she knew it by the way he looked at her. Just as he was certain she'd liked it that he'd won the race even if she didn't say so. Thirty four years together and they still fancied the pants off each other. Sex had always been great between them, first as excited teenagers, then in heightened reunions after his stints in Kuwait, secretive once Gerard came along, and openly joyful now that their son was away at University.

Gerard ambled over just at that moment, shoulder-length hair bobbing in time with the satchel slung over his shoulder, Gerard's arms flung out in his usual gregarious manner:

'Hey, I missed you two finish?'

Evan smiled:

'You missed your dad beating me another year. I would have thought an aspiring journo like you would be there to get the winner's first thoughts.'

'You two coming first and second is old news.'

Gerard looked over toward the Cancer Trust stall:

'I was over there talking to the people who set up this run, about the work they do.'

That was his son, thought Ryan. He'd talk to anyone, unlike himself. Ryan guessed journalism was the right career for Gerard, but who knew if there was any work out there.

The Evening Post guys came over to take a photo, Ryan holding up a cheque for the amount raised in the Run for Cancer. Coincidentally his parents had both died of the disease a year before in quick succession, but he'd done the run for the last twenty years without having any personal reason.

The Trust couldn't do much for his parents as it all happened so quickly. A heavy smoker, it was no surprise that his dad got cancer. It must have been all the passive smoking in the small terraced house that did for his mum.

While Gerard talked to the journalist from the Post, Ryan followed Sandra and Evan who had gravitated toward the café. Both had stopped at Huw's table and were talking with the bank manager.

Huw was in his Sunday casuals, a polo t-shirt tucked into his jeans. He wasn't overweight, but his rugby playing days were long gone and Ryan knew it wasn't muscle that always made Huw's clothes too tight.

Huw made as if to shake hands with Ryan but thought better of it, presumably not wanting to get sweaty:

'If I were allowed to bet on the run instead of sponsoring it, I'd have placed my money on you, boy.'

Ryan looked at Huw blankly, thinking they were both fifty years old and Huw still used the term 'boy', only out of the office of course. Huw was a chameleon and Ryan knew he altered his speech depending on the setting and who he was speaking to.

Huw glanced at the ensemble, his eyes lingering a little too long on Sandra's cleavage:

'Successful businessman, beautiful younger wife…'

Sandra rolled her eyes. Huw knew full well she was only a year younger, but he was unabashed as he gestured over toward Gerard:

'…Son at university, you deserve a medal Ryan – though you've probably already got one of those too. Bloody pin up boy for the city you are.'

Huw glanced at Evan:

'No offence to our most prominent policeman.'

Evan exchanged glances with Ryan, who simply shrugged. You had to be careful with Huw as, behind the smarmy charm, his words were always barbed, Huw having a knack for getting under people's skin. Huw smiled as he stood and tossed a ten pound note onto the table, making sure both Ryan and Evan got a good long look at his bulging wallet.

'I'm off. Good to see you all.'

Ryan saw that Huw's latte was untouched. It was Sandra's favourite type of coffee but too milky for Ryan so he could understand Huw not drinking it. But then why buy it? It was Huw's ten pound note that Sandra noticed:

'That's a tip and a half.'

Huw shrugged and tossed another ten pound note onto the table:

'They need all the money they can get at present.'

He winked at Sandra:

'I don't like to tell tales out of school but on the Q.T. they might not be around much longer, times are tough and the bank may have to foreclose.'

Huw smiled gratingly:

'You never heard it from me.'

It was typical Huw, thought Ryan, always playing the big man. Ryan meant to keep silent but couldn't help comment:

'So who did we hear it from then?'

Huw opened his mouth to answer, but was confused, not getting that Ryan was making fun of his patter. He turned to go, then stopped and looked back at Ryan as if he'd just remembered:

'I'll see you on Tuesday, yeah?'

Ryan's face hardened as Huw smiled and sauntered off, not waiting for an answer. Sandra frowned at Ryan:

'You're seeing him Tuesday?'

Ryan waved a dismissive hand.

'Annual meeting with the bank.'

'Everything okay?'

'It's nothing to worry about. I just don't like talking shop on my day off.'

Evan snorted:

'Huw never tires of talking about money. Did you see him flash the cash, like we're supposed to be impressed? The guy was an arsehole at school and he hasn't changed much since.'

Sandra smiled thinly.

'Makes the world go around.'

Sidling up to the group, Gerard joined in:

'That's what people want us to think, but it doesn't have to be that way...'

Sandra interrupted her son:

'Do you think there's some kind of magic fairy that funds you to live in London?'

Ryan chided his wife:

'Give him a break Sandra, he's going to become a famous journalist, make loads of cash and look after us in our old age.'

'I'll say it again, because you two never seem to listen to a word I say, but with his grades he should be in medical school.'

Evan smiled:

'I'll leave you to it. I've got to pick up Julie from that

Sofa Store, the one having a closing down sale.'

Sandra shook her head:

'There won't be many shops left open soon.'

She looked pointedly at Ryan, who shifted his gaze to stare out across the Bay. Evan grabbed a handshake with Ryan, looking for eye contact as he said:

'Don't forget that drink we're going to have.'

Ryan nodded, his eyes darting away once again to the yachts gliding on the horizon. Evan jogged off, leaving Ryan with his wife and son. Sandra linked arms with both Ryan and Gerard, propelling them along the promenade. The three of them headed towards Mumbles, rivulets of seawater lit up on the vast sand beach. As Gerard got back into his anti-capitalist diatribe, Ryan exhaled in happiness. Strolling along Swansea Bay on a sunny Sunday morning with his family, you couldn't beat it. He couldn't let his worries ruin this time. There were plenty of things to worry about, the Tuesday bank meeting being one. But Ryan was determined not to deal with them until Monday.

Read more at www.iponymous.com

17/5/19

20390894R00123

Printed in Great Britain
by Amazon